DON'T LOOK
30 TALES OF TERROR

CHILLING TALES FOR THE CAMPFIRE
BOOK THREE

BLAIR DANIELS

CONTENTS

We Have Been Playing Hide And Seek For Three Days	1
The Light Switches Are On Different Walls	14
Rules Of The Farm	20
My Neighbor Got A Dog. I Don't Think It's A Dog	45
I Used Chatgpt And I Regret Everything	59
My Milkshake Brings Something Terrible To The Yard	66
The Same Man Is Appearing Behind My Friends On Zoom	72
23Andme Says I Have A Second Mother	79
Never Have I Ever	93
Facebook Is Showing Me Memories I Don't Remember Having	98
If You See A Light On The Water, Run	103
Side Effects	113
Streetlights Blinking	119
The Porcelain Lady	125
Warning: Contents May Cause Happiness	135
Strip Mall	140
Cheese	144
Advice For My Wedding Night	151
Signaling In The Lake	156
Good Luck Means You'll Die	162
All The Cells In My Body Are Dead	167
Caution: Falling Rocks	181
The Town Of Chelm	189
Voices In The Woods	199
Photos Of Me Sleeping	203

Afterimage	210
Ocd	215
I Visit My Dead Mother Every Night	222
Sos	233
I Babysat A Parrot. It Said Disturbing Things	239

WE HAVE BEEN PLAYING HIDE AND SEEK FOR THREE DAYS

My wife and I have been playing hide and seek for three days straight

posted by B____ on May 26, 2023

I don't know what to do. In the past 72 hours my life has been turned upside-down. Our family has been thrown into chaos. My wife is missing, and I fear she'll never return.

Let me start from the beginning.

My wife and I started playing hide and seek with our two young kids. However, they're a little too young to hide effectively--they always hide in the same spot, every time. So we've found it's more fun for one of us parents to hide, and then the rest of us seek.

I've hidden from my wife and kids just by standing completely still in the corner of a dark room. It's amazing how our brains are programmed to see things that move. My wife gets a little more creative, but it's hard for us to do anything too elaborate because the kids are not very cooperative in waiting for us to hide.

On Tuesday evening after work, we decided to play. My wife decided to hide first. I counted down from 10 with the kids holed up in the downstairs office.

"Ready or not, here I come!"

The kids bounded out of the room like wild dogs. I followed, slowly, trying to get a sense of where my wife was hiding. I'd often try to figure out what room she was hiding in first, to gently guide the kids so that we wouldn't find her too soon, or spend too long looking for her.

I saw her when I entered the living room. She was crouched behind the couch--I could see a bit of her elbow poking out from behind the upholstery. The kids walked right past her, too intent on checking the kitchen.

I waited for them to return. As they walked back in and rounded the couch, I waited for them to squeal in delight.

Except they didn't. Confused, I approached the couch--

She wasn't there.

Huh. Maybe I'd just seen a tag or something poking out. Or maybe she'd moved her hiding spot. Wouldn't be the first time. As I said, she's more creative at this than I am.

So we moved on. We checked all the usual spots-- underneath the shelving in the garage, behind the kitchen door, even in the lower kitchen cabinets.

She wasn't in any of those spots.

Maybe she went upstairs. I hadn't heard her go upstairs, but she can creep pretty quietly. I walked along the hallways, the kids in tow. "Jessie," I called, in a sing-song voice. "We're going to find you!"

Gotcha.

Our bedroom door was open. And there was a long, Jess-shaped lump under the covers. "Let's check Mom and Dad's bedroom!" I said to the kids. Pattering footsteps as they charged behind me.

I reached for the light switch--flicked on the lights-- then grabbed the hem of the comforter and yanked it off.

My heart dropped.

The bed was empty.

I stared down in confusion. *It must've just been bunched up weirdly? But I could've sworn it looked like a person under there... The rough shape of someone in a fetal position, legs bent, back curved...*

I backed out of the room. The kids and I went downstairs. "Jess," I called out. "We can't find you. Come on out."

Nothing.

The kids lost interest. They bounded into the family room and began playing with their toys. I was about to call out again, when I noticed that the chain of the basement door lock was disengaged.

Aha.

As I approached, my heart hammered in my chest. I knew she was waiting on the other side. Waiting to jump out at me and give me a heart attack. She'd done that before.

I took a deep breath and swung open the door--

She wasn't there.

Damp air wafted up from the basement. I clicked on the light. "Jess?" I called out.

No answer.

"The kids aren't playing anymore," I called down. "And you shouldn't be hiding down there anyway. These stairs are too dangerous." Nothing. I turned, about to close the door—but then something caught my eye.

Black hair. Poking through the gap between the stairs, about halfway down.

She's hiding under the stairs.

I stepped down. The wood creaked under my weight. The hair glistened below me in the dim yellow light. I continued down the steps, avoiding stepping on her hair, until I was standing on the concrete floor.

I whirled around—

"Aha!"

But the space under the stairs was empty.

My blood ran cold. "Jess, this isn't funny!" I shouted. "Stop playing games with me!"

A footstep sounded behind me. I whirled around.

The naked bulb in the ceiling only lit half the basement. The other half, where we had rows and rows of storage boxes, was in near-total darkness.

But...

I squinted, trying to make it out. In the murky darkness... behind a stack of boxes, in the corner... I thought I could see her standing there.

I could only see her in my peripheral vision. Like how you can only see dim stars when you're not looking right at them, because of how your optic cells are arranged. I focused on one of the storage boxes, really stared at it; and when I did, I realized I could see her pale calves, extending up into the darkness.

And, as I stood there, I realized I could hear her breathing.

"I can see you there," I said, my voice wavering. "Why are you being so weird? The kids aren't even playing anymore. So come out. Please?"

Deep in the pit of my stomach, I knew there was something wrong. Something horribly wrong. So I chickened out.

"I'm going upstairs. You can join me when you're ready."

I headed for the stairs. But halfway there, the bulb flickered—and went out.

Total darkness surrounded me. I stretched my hands out, blindly groping into the darkness. They only fell on air. I frantically pawed through the air, searching for something, anything—

My fingers caught in something.

Hair.

I screamed and yanked my hands back. Then I ran blindly into the darkness—but something glanced off me. I shoved at it—I heard a dull *thwack*—and then I kept running. The side of the banister caught me straight in the chest. Panting, I felt my way to the stairs and climbed them as fast as I could.

Then I locked the door to the basement and frantically ran to my kids.

They were fine. But as I hugged them, I couldn't get the horrible thought out of my mind. The hair I'd felt... it was higher than my eye level. About six, six-and-a-half feet off the ground.

Jess is only 5' 2".

The police searched the entire house. My wife isn't here.

They searched the backyard and patrolled in a three mile radius. They came up empty-handed. It's like she disappeared off the face of the earth.

Except.

Last night, as I rolled over in bed, *I swear* my fingers touched something warm.

My wife and I have been playing hide and seek - Update
posted by B___ on June 24, 2023

It's been a while since I updated, and I'm sorry. But my life has been hell. I don't even trust my own sanity anymore. I don't know what's real and what's not.

But I do know one thing for sure.

Jess, the love of my life, is gone.

When she'd been missing for three days, I did everything I could to find her. I stapled MISSING posters to telephone poles. I called friends and family, people she could've escaped to. Even though her car was still in the driveway. Even though I *knew* she must be somewhere in the house. I soldiered on and pretended this was an average missing persons case.

But things only got worse.

On the morning of day 7, I opened our closet to get dressed. As I scanned the hanging shirts, looking for my purple button-down, I noticed something in my peripheral vision. Something beige-colored, poking out from under the sleeve of Jess's flannel shirt.

I couldn't be sure, but from the brief glimpse I got— it looked like a finger.

Every muscle in my body froze. My heart began to pound. My eyes snapped on it—just in time to see a hint of movement in the limp, hanging sleeve. As if there was *something in there,* pulling itself up, coiling further into the shirt.

I leapt forward and thrust my arms into the clothes. Pushed them back and forth. But there was nothing. Heart throbbing in my ears, I ripped shirts off their hangers and threw them on the ground. I didn't stop until all the clothes were heaped in a pile on the floor.

But, of course, the closet was empty.

I stood there, panting, feeling like a madman. *I must've imagined it. I must've...* But every time I closed my eyes, I saw the movement in the sleeve. Of something pulling back up into it. And it made my stomach turn.

For a few days, I was able to keep it together. I stuck to the routine of sleep, eat, work, pick kids up, spend time with them, go to bed. I focused on comforting them. Telling them that everything would be okay. It was hard to answer their questions—"where's Mommy?" "when will Mommy be home?"—but I comforted them as best I could. The three of us were in this together. At least we had each other.

But the peace was short-lived.

I was watching TV after the kids went to sleep. I got up to get another drink—and saw something poking out from the wall, by the stairs.

It was on the second stair. Just a little black blob, that my brain knew wasn't supposed to be there. *What is that?* I got up and stepped closer, the voices on the TV growing distant as I focused on it. *Did the kids drop some food, or a sock, or something?*

I got closer—and then froze.

I recognized it. The shiny black satin, the edge of the bow... It was one of Jess's high heels. And now, as I got closer, I could see a bit of flesh poking out above the edge of the shoe. And a shadow, stretching out along the hardwood floor.

She's standing there.

"J—Jess?" I asked, my voice barely above a whisper.

Silence.

I stepped closer, staring at the shoe. At that bit of pale flesh, the top of her foot, sticking out above the curved edge. I grabbed the side of the wall for balance, and then as fast as I could, swung out into the foyer.

Nothing.

No one was standing on the stairs.

I backed away. I felt dizzy. *Maybe I imagined it. I have had three drinks...* But deep down, I knew I didn't imagine it. Just like I didn't imagine seeing Jess in the basement that night. Or feeling that hair in the darkness. I wasn't crazy... at least, I didn't think so. Then again, if I were crazy, I probably wouldn't know I was.

I forced the incident out of my mind. I had to. I had to keep it together, for my Ava and Henry. They'd already lost one parent. They couldn't lose two. So I just focused everything I had on helping them, comforting them, loving them.

But then there was that horrible night, two weeks ago.

"Daddy, I'm scared," Ava said as she walked into my room.

It was almost eleven. Way past Ava's bedtime. I groaned, thinking how cranky she'd be when I had to wake her up for school in the morning. "Why are you scared?" I asked, getting out of bed.

"There's a monster under my bed."

All the blood drained out of my face.

Normally, those words wouldn't scare a parent. Kids always think there are monsters under the bed. It's practically a cliché. But going through everything with Jess... my heart sunk into my stomach like an anchor.

"I heard it breathing."

My heart plummeted further. "Okay, sweetheart," I finally said, forcing a smile on my face. "I'll check it out for you."

The two of us walked towards her bedroom. My heart throbbed in my ears. When we got to the doorway, I paused. "Um... you go to your brother's room, okay? And I'll check it out."

She skipped off to his room, and I was left alone.

At first, nothing seemed amiss. I could make out most of the room in the dim light from the mermaid nightlight at her bedside. The space under the bed, however, was pitch black.

I swallowed.

Then I slowly got on my hands and knees.

The darkness under the bed was pure black. But when I actually lowered my head to the floor, I saw straight through to the other side. Her pile of stuffed animals and dolls, all thrown together in a heap. The bottom of her unicorn poster. The shaggy purple rug.

I began to get up—

And froze.

No. No no no.

There was hair. Hanging off the edge of the bed.

I lay there, frozen. Black spots danced in my vision. The hair didn't move as I stared at it—it didn't disappear or go away. *Is Jess... lying on the bed?* I sucked in a breath. My heart pounded so hard I felt dizzy.

Slowly, holding my breath, I pushed myself up. My eyes peeked over the top of the bed. First I saw the covers, then Ava's pillow, then—

Oh, for fuck's sake.

Ava's Frozen doll, Anna, was laying at the edge of the bed. Her hair cascaded over the edge, looking almost black in the dim light.

I grabbed the stupid doll and put it on the pillow. Then I grabbed the comforter and shook it out, laying it on the bed and smoothing it out. *These damn kids. Gonna give me a heart attack someday, I swear.* "Ava!" I called, turning around. "Your room's fi—"

My breath caught in my throat.

The air vent. Near the floor. Between the metal slats —two eyes glimmered in the darkness.

I expected myself to scream. To run. But I'd had enough of this thing, whatever it was, tormenting me. I scrambled over to the vent. "Hey—*hey!*" I screamed. My voice echoed against the metal. "Come back here! *What did you do to Jess?!*"

Soft thumping sounds. As it crawled deeper into the house. And then... nothing.

I let out a shuddering breath. Slowly, I stood up, my heart pounding. I stepped out into the hallway—

And then I heard the screams.

Seeing that *thing* in the air vents was nothing

compared to the fear I felt when I heard my children scream. I raced down the hallway, every part of my body in panic mode. "Ava! Henry!" I shouted, my feet pounding underneath me.

The door to Henry's room hung open.

I burst inside. Ava was cowered with Henry, who'd just woken up. Both of them were staring behind me. At the shadows behind the bedroom door. I grabbed the doorknob and, in one swift motion, swung it open.

Just in time to see a lock of dark hair disappear back into the air vent.

"Come on. We're getting out of here." I picked up Henry, grabbed Ava's hand, and we raced for the stairs. Metallic thumping sounded through the walls all around us, as if it were following us in the air ducts. Frantically trying to prevent our escape.

But we made it out to the car. And then we were pulling out of the driveway, tires screeching against the road.

Two days ago I put the house up for sale. We can't live here anymore. I don't know what's living in my house now, but it isn't Jess. My wife is gone.

I told the real estate agent everything that happened. It didn't feel right letting another family buy this house, only to be tormented by this thing. But she just looked at me like I was crazy.

And maybe I am.

But I know now that my kids have seen it too. Heard

it. Felt its presence, crawling and slithering within the bowels of our home.

So this is the only way I know of to warn you. If you're looking for a house... and come across a white house with burgundy shutters, behind a picket fence on a dead end street, in Franklin, Pennsylvania...

Don't buy it.

THE LIGHT SWITCHES ARE ON DIFFERENT WALLS

I've lived in this house for the past 23 years.

Just like the past eight-thousand nights, as I was going to bed, I reached out to turn off the light switch in the stairwell. The one right at the top of the stairs, on the left-hand side as I go up.

Except it wasn't there.

I stopped and looked down. My hand was pressed against blank wall. I turned around, and saw the switch on the *other* side of the stairwell.

Huh?

Had the switch always been on that side? It had been so long, I'd never really paid attention to where exactly the light switch was. It was pure muscle memory. Reach out… turn off the light… go into my bedroom.

I looked down. "Oh." I was holding a freshly-laundered sheet and pillowcase in my left hand. That stopped me from turning off the light. Instead of switching hands, my muscle memory just told my brain "Hey! Go ahead and turn off the light with your *other* hand!"

Silly brain.

There was nothing wrong.

I opened the door to my bedroom and started pulling the fitted sheet over the mattress. I pulled the cloth straight, straightening out the wrinkles, neatly tucking the corners underneath. I repeated it four times, then with a sigh, got up and went into the bathroom. I reached to flick on the light—

Blank wall.

What the...

I extended my other arm. After a second of fumbling, my fingers found the switch and flipped it on. I scowled at myself in the mirror. At the reflection of my bony hand, frozen on the light switch.

I'm pretty sure the light switch was on the other side. Next to the towel rack.

Not... there.

I walked over to the counter and pulled the bobby pins out of my hair. Then pulled it all up into a ponytail, securing it with a neon green hairtie. I reached down for the drawer to pull out my toothpaste.

Except my fingers grabbed empty air.

I looked down—to find the drawer pull a few inches lower than I expected it to be. "Geez, what's wrong with me today?" I muttered under my breath. I grabbed my toothpaste out of the drawer, squirted it on my toothbrush, and furiously brushed my teeth.

I bent over the sink and cupped my hands, filling

them with water. I sucked it up, swishing, and spit it out. Straightened back up—

Huh?

Over my shoulder, in the mirror, the fitted sheet sat bunched up on top of the mattress.

My heart dropped. *I definitely put that sheet on.* Then I frowned. *Did I? Or did I just... think... about doing it?* I turned around, staring at the bunched fabric. The cute little green polka dots distorted with the wrinkles.

Then I shook my head and walked over to the bed. Flapped the sheet in the air, then lined up the corners. Pulled it taut, tucking each corner underneath.

"Looking good."

I walked over to the windows and closed them. Locked them. Pulled down the blinds, then pulled the curtains over them. Without the light of the moon, the room was pitch dark, save for the sliver of golden light spilling out from the bathroom door.

Leaving the bathroom light on so I wouldn't trip over myself, I sat down on the bed and turned on the desk lamp. Pulled my Kindle off the nightstand and opened the novel I'd been reading. Some dramedy about two very different women switching bodies. I read for several minutes—but then something caught my eye.

The mirror.

In the full-length mirror across from the bed, I could see my reflection: blankets cozily wrapped around me, cup of water on the nightstand, Kindle in hand. Except there was something horribly, horribly wrong.

My hair was down.

No. I put my hair up in a ponytail. In the bathroom. I

was sure of it—otherwise, I would've gotten my hair wet in the sink when I brushed my teeth.

Unless... maybe I absentmindedly put it back down while I was reading?

The neon-green hairtie sat on the nightstand. I grabbed it and quickly put my hair back up. Then I stared at the mirror. My reflection stared back, eyes wide.

You're just tired.

You've had a hell of a day. Hell of a week. The presentation at work, fixing the cracked window in the basement all by yourself. You just need a good sleep.

I reached over and turned off the lamp.

Darkness enveloped me. And it felt somehow... *too* dark. Usually there was light from *something*, even if it was just the blinking white light from my laptop, indicating sleep mode. But this was just pure darkness. Thick, heavy darkness like a fog, filling the entire room.

Go to sleep. You need sleep.

I cuddled up to my pillow, closed my eyes, and began to fall asleep—

My eyes shot open.

The light.

I'd left the light on in the bathroom.

And now it was off.

I pulled myself up out of bed. "Hello? Is anyone there?"

Oh, good idea, Hannah. Announce yourself like every victim in a slasher movie ever.

Groping in the darkness, I felt for my phone. I'd left it on the nightstand. Which should've been a foot or two to my right. But as I continued to feel, my hand only fell on empty air.

Where the hell is the nightstand?!

I walked forward with slow, halting steps. Then my toe collided with something. I hissed in pain, but reached down and finally found the sleek smooth metal of my phone.

I turned on the flashlight.

And my blood ran cold.

My bed. The nightstand. It was all on the *left* side of the room, not the right. I stared at it, my heart pounding in my chest. The white light jittered across the wall as my hand shook.

I turned around, towards the bathroom—

But I was staring at the windows. The curtains closed tight. I whipped around, and there was the door to the bathroom—on the *other* side of the room.

"What the fuck?!"

I ran to the bedroom door. Turned the knob. Swung the door open and raced down the hallway—

The stairs.

They didn't lead down.

They led *up*.

My flashlight followed the wooden steps as they went up—turned ninety-degrees at the landing—and then continued upwards. At the top, there was a shut door. A door I'd seen a million times.

The door to my basement.

A dream. This has got to be a dream. I pinched myself, screamed, tried to force myself awake. But I was still standing in the hallway. The hallway that led *up* to the basement door.

I raced up the stairs and opened the door. Or tried to—it only opened a few inches before the chain lock caught. I thrust my entire weight against the door, pulling the chain taut. But the door wouldn't open any further.

"Let me out!"

Light blinked on. On the other side of the door.

And through the crack... I could see something. Something familiar. A hallway with a cuckoo clock. Cream-colored walls. An opening that led to a small, wallpapered kitchen.

It was *my* house.

And standing in the kitchen was a woman. A woman with dark hair pulled back with a neon-green ponytail holder.

Me.

She held a toolbox and a garbage bag. Something like glass clanked against each other with each step she took. Then she disappeared around the bend, towards the garage.

"Help!" I screamed. "Help me!"

But no one came.

I've tried calling the police. Tried calling my mom, my friends, *anyone*. It never goes through though. It seems like I have some sort of internet connection, though, and I'm not even sure where this will be seen. But I hope someone will see it.

And I hope you can help me.

RULES OF THE FARM

A few miles north of me, there's a little family-owned farm. The family takes a vacation in July, though, and they posted a job listing for a caretaker. My job would include feeding the animals, making sure the irrigation is working, and harvesting some crops. It's a small operation, so it's not fields and fields of stuff. Plus, they were offering *two thousand dollars*. At the time, that seemed like an amazing deal.

Now, I'm not so sure.

See, the Gershons left me detailed instructions in the envelope, along with half of the stipend. And as I sat down to read it, I realized that it sounded a little... strange.

Dear Emily,

Thank you for taking care of our farm! To ensure your safety and happiness (and the animals'!), we've included a list of instructions and tasks.

1. Please feed the goats and chickens at 6 AM sharp. They get pretty cranky if it's not on time :)

2. You will need to prune off the floricanes in the raspberry patch. To do this, cut the canes (branches) that are "woody" and have already fruited. Wear thick gloves because there are thorns. If you do get cut, immediately head inside and call Dr. Lively to make sure your wound is not infected.

3. The sunflower field is easy to maintain and brings beauty to our farm. However, if you ever see a sunflower that isn't facing the same direction as the others, immediately head inside. Do not return to the sunflower field until the following day.

4. The farm is, as you know, surrounded by forest. Sometimes we get coyotes, foxes, or other wild animals prowling about the grounds at night. Don't worry—the animal pens are completely secure and there is no need to check on the animals if you hear anything at night. In fact, we recommend you do not leave the farmhouse between sunset and sunrise.

5. Do not enter the corn maze. Even if you hear noises coming from the maze, that sound like a child crying, do not enter. The corn maze is not open to visitors yet. It's most likely the bobcats in the woods.

6. Do not be alarmed if you see the goats awake in the middle of the night. They are semi-nocturnal and often wake up to roam, graze, or use the bathroom.

7. You may help yourself to any of the fruits or

vegetables you harvest, however, do not eat the apples from the northwest corner of the orchard.

    8. We no longer use scarecrows. If you see one, please return to the house, lock all the doors, and close all the curtains. Stay inside until the following morning.

    9. Make sure to always stock the farmstand twice a day: in the morning, and again in the afternoon. At night, take all unsold produce inside and store it in the refrigerator.

    10. We do not own any pigs.

    Thank you so very much, Emily! – The Gershons

    I glanced out the window. The sun was hanging low over the trees, orange rays filtering through the forest. *Dammit, if I'm not supposed to be out after dark because of the wolves or whatever, I better get cracking.*

    I walked over to the goats first. They huddled close to me as I filled their food bins, staring at me with their weird slit-pupils. I tried to get it done as quickly as possible—goats, honestly, freaked me out a little bit. As I hurried away, one with black-and-white fur pushed its little face through the fence. *Maaaaaa,* it bleated, staring at me.

    The chickens were more skeptical of me, staring at me and letting out long *baaaawwwwwks?* as they bobbed their heads. As soon as they realized I had food, though, they came over and pecked the ground. They were pretty cute, actually.

    I turned back towards the house—

    I froze.

    Across the field from me stood the field of sunflowers. Bright golden petals and dark centers, swaying slightly in the wind. But while all of them tilted away from me, facing the dying sun, one of them—near the edge of the field—was instead facing me.

I stared at its pitch black center. *Didn't the note say something about that? Go inside, if one of the sunflowers is pointing a different way?*

I locked up the chicken gate. Then I strode across the grass towards the old farmhouse, still carrying the bag of chicken feed. I was halfway to the house when I turned around again.

I wish I hadn't.

The sunflower was still facing me. Even though, based on my path, it shouldn't have been.

I picked up my pace towards the house. *Oh, come on, what do you think's gonna happen? That sunflower is gonna chase after you and murder you?* My brain knew it was stupid, but there was something instinctual, a gut feeling, that forced my legs to pump harder. I didn't even bother dropping the feed off at the shed—I raced into the house and locked all the doors.

Phew. Safe.

I took a final glance out at the sunflower. Then I went into the tiny kitchen and started some water boiling for pasta. By the time I was sitting down to eat, I was shaking my head. *So stupid. Afraid of a sunflower.*

Something woke me up in the middle of the night.

I sat up, my neck aching from the crappy pillow

they'd left for me. I looked around my tiny bedroom, but nothing seemed amiss. Well, of course there were things amiss, like the peeling paint and the light bulb that flickered and the clogged toilet. But nothing *different*.

I yawned and checked my phone. 3:12 AM. Sighing, I settled back into sleep.

But before I drifted off, I heard it. A small, high-pitched noise.

Coming from outside.

I slowly forced myself out of bed and walked over to the window. Underneath me, the farm sprawled out into the darkness—but it was distorted in the old glass, shapes and colors bleeding into each other like running paint. I flipped the window lock and pushed it open, the wood squeaking loudly in my ears.

I listened.

Silence. Then—

"Help me."

A voice. A child's voice.

Coming from the direction of the cornfield.

That's no fucking bobcat.

My blood ran cold. I stared out into the darkness, at the cornfield on the edge of the woods. Hoping that it was just some lingering dream or something. But as I stood there, the cool summer breeze wafting into the room, I heard it again.

"Please. Help me."

The voice wavered, as if the child was crying. I squinted into the darkness, staring at the cornfield. *I have to go out there.* I remembered the Gershon's rule—but there was *no way* this was an animal.

"Hey! I'm coming, don't worry!" I shouted out the window.

Silence.

And then a rustling sound. I squinted at the cornfield—and I could see the stalks moving, as something moved within them. "Stay where you are!" I shouted into the darkness. "I'm coming to get you!"

The cornstalks continued to move.

And every muscle in my body froze.

The amount of corn moving... there was no *way* it was just a small child in there. The corn was swaying, dancing, roiling in an area maybe ten feet across.

And it was making its way towards the edge of the field.

Rapidly.

I shut the window. Then I closed the blinds, my heart hammering in my chest. I raced downstairs and checked the locks. And then, finally—when I was sure I was safe—I called the police. But they wouldn't even come out. "There are no missing children in the area, and what you saw was most likely a bear," they explained calmly.

I think they must know all about the Gershon's farm.

I triple-checked the locks, wedged a chair under the doorknob, and tried to sleep. But I spent most of the night awake, listening the *snaps* and *rustles* of the cornstalks, waiting for dawn.

6 AM came all too early. The alarm blared in my ears and I forced myself out of bed, groaning. The sun had just crested over the hill, and the sky was lit with the pale grey of dawn. I could hear the rooster crowing already.

I looked out the window. Scanned the farm. But everything looked normal. All the sunflowers were facing halfway towards me, in direction of the rising sun. The cornfield was still. The chickens were milling about the coop, pecking the ground.

I went downstairs, grabbed the bag of feed I'd never put away, and went out to the coop.

The chickens were probably the only part of the farm I liked. The fat little hens ran towards me as I poured the food onto the ground. Making happy noises, they pecked it up. I locked the gate and started over the hill, towards the shed, to get the goat feed.

That's when I heard it.

Oink.

I stopped in my tracks. *The Gershon's note said they didn't own any pigs.*

Oink.

The note didn't say anything about avoiding the pigs, though. So I was free to go fetch the goat feed. *Right?* I started walking again, up the hill.

Oink.

And that's when I realized there was something off about the sound. It almost sounded... human? Like a person saying "oink," instead of an actual animal sound. For a second I had a weird mental image of a naked man covered in his own filth, crouching on the ground, saying *oink* over and over.

Oink.

I shook my head and continued up the hill. And when I got to the top, I saw the source of the noise: a fat, pink pig, standing in the grass. I let out a breath of relief. *See? It's just an ordinary pig.* I passed the pig, ignoring it completely, and opened the shed. Put the chicken feed back. Pulled out the goat feed. Started back up the hill—

I stopped dead as my eyes fell on the pig.

Its face.

It almost looked... *human.*

Its fleshy, pink snout was shorter than it should be. Its curled little ears sat low and flat on its head. And its eyes... they weren't round and beady, but almond-shaped, like a person's. With dark pupils that stared up at me in a way that suggested intelligence.

The feed bag fell out of my hands. I stumbled back. But the pig didn't advance. It just... *stared...* at me with its human-eyes.

I backed away, keeping my eyes on it. Slowly walked around it so that I was going back towards the house. When I got over the hill, and that horrible little face was finally out of my sight, I whipped around and broke into a run.

"What. The fuck. Was that?!" I panted to myself, as I locked the front door behind me.

Not knowing what else to do, I pulled out my phone and called the police. But when they picked up, I wasn't sure what to say. "I... uh," I started. "Found a pig that doesn't look like a pig. On the farm. The Gershon's farm—"

"Did you touch the pig?" the officer cut in.

"I... what?"

"Did you have any contact with the pig, any at all?"

"No..."

"Good. We'll send an officer out to deal with it."

Fifteen minutes later, I saw a police car pull up the driveway. They asked me where I'd seen it, then told me to stay inside. I went over to the window and watched them walk up the hill, then disappear. A minute passed; then a shrill squeal erupted in the silence.

Five minutes later, the officers reappeared, carrying a large black plastic bag that swung with each step. "Hey—*hey!*" I called out, as they headed for the cruiser. "What—what *was* that thing?"

The officers glanced at each other.

"Rabies," the female officer said, while the male stuffed the bag into the backseat. "A bunch of rabid pigs have been showing up in this area. Gonna send it off to get tested. Good thing you didn't touch it."

Before I could ask her more questions, she hopped into the driver's side. And then they were gone.

I stared out the window, utterly perplexed. *Why didn't the Gershons tell me to stay away from the pigs?*

After the debacle with the pig, I decided to take it easy. I made a wholesome breakfast, read a few chapters of the thriller I was working through, and called my boyfriend.

Around 11 AM, though, I realized I'd forgotten to stock the farmstand.

It was still technically morning, so I ran out into the field, filled my hod with zucchini and tomatoes, and ran down the driveway as fast as I could without spilling any of the produce.

But as the little farmstand came into view, I saw that there was already someone waiting. I checked my watch: 11:49 AM.

"I'm so sorry," I breathed as I spread the produce out on the wooden table. "I was supposed to get this out earlier but, there was a pig, and it just..." Something made me stop rambling. I glanced up—to see that the person standing there was a little... odd.

He was an old man, probably about six feet tall, and very thin. He wore, surprisingly, a crisp black suit and an old-timey bowler hat in the sweltering heat. He was smiling at me, but his teeth were deeply yellow and crooked, and his eyes were sunken back in his skull. Nothing unnatural about him—just a slightly creepy-looking old guy—but in a way, he reminded me of the creepy dudes from that one *Buffy the Vampire* episode where they take away everyone's voices.

"So... what are you looking for today?" I asked, when he didn't move to take any of the produce.

"The Gershons aren't here?"

I shook my head. "Won't be back for two weeks."

"Hmm," he said, thoughtfully. "They didn't tell me they were leaving."

"Oh, you know them?"

He let out a small chuckle. "You could say that."

I waited for him to either take produce or leave. But he didn't do either. He just stood there, looking at me. The way his blue eyes cut into mine made a chill run down my spine. It wasn't a predatory or sexual stare—it felt more like he was examining me, studying me, trying to read every tilt of my head and blink of my eyes.

It made me extremely uncomfortable.

"So, uh, are you interested in any of this? The tomatoes looked really good today," I said, trying to not sound nervous. "Or if you're looking for something else, I can go pick it for you."

"Only the Gershons can provide what I'm looking for."

"Okay, well uh, I'm going back up to the farm. If you change your mind, the prices are listed on the whiteboard, and you just leave the money in the box." I shot him a fake smile, turned around, and headed up the hill as quickly as I could without seeming weird.

But then he said something that made my blood run cold.

"Emily?"

I never told him my name.

The smartest thing would've been to run. But instead, I turned around. He wasn't chasing me—he was still standing at the farmstand, ten yards from me.

"I wouldn't trust the Gershons if I were you," he called out.

Then he turned on his heel and strode away.

As I watched him go, I realized there wasn't any car parked at the bottom of the driveway. He just turned onto the old country road and walked away. I watched him until he rounded the bend and disappeared from sight.

I retreated into the house, checked all the locks, and decided I would spend the rest of the day inside—at least, until it was time to feed the animals and stock the farmstand again.

When I fed the goats that evening, they still seemed mad at me from the morning. With all the pig business, I hadn't gotten their morning meal to them until nearly 10 AM, and as I entered the pen they eyed me warily. *Maaaaaa*, a brown one bleated, with a look of betrayal in its slit-pupil eyes.

My last task of the day was picking up the unsold produce. I hurried down the driveway, garden hod in my arms, an audiobook playing through my earbuds. The sun hung low in the sky, casting shadows that stretched across the driveway before me. The sun wasn't setting yet—that wouldn't be for another hour—but it still made me nervous.

Most of the produce was gone, but I grabbed the three remaining zucchini and put them in the hod. Then I turned around and hurried back up the hill as fast as I could.

But when I crested the hill, I saw something in the fields that made my heart stop.

A scarecrow.

Its arms stretched out at its sides. Its head hung limply on its shoulders. I couldn't see it in detail—it was too far away—but I could see its silhouette clearly. I immediately broke into a sprint.

Just get inside. You'll be fine.

I focused on the white door. It was still so far away. But I forced myself to stare at it, to keep my eyes away from the scarecrow. *Just run. As fast as you can.*

And I made it.

I slammed the door shut. Drew the deadbolt. Closed all the curtains. Checked all the other locks. And then, I collapsed onto the couch and called my boyfriend, Derek.

"You have to come here," I told him. "There's someone out there and I ran inside but I think…" I rambled on in incoherent sentences, until he interrupted me.

"Wait, slow down. You think there's someone out there?"

"Yes."

"Are you *sure?*"

Derek was a good man. But he often thought I was being a little too paranoid, a little too scared. When I insisted I was being followed home from work, he told me it was probably nothing, and just some guy walking the same route as me. When I heard sounds in the middle of the night, he insisted it was the house settling. When I watched true crime shows and told him how we need to do X or Y so we don't fall victim to a crime like that, he'd just laugh. It wasn't intentionally mean, but in these moments it was painfully obvious he'd grown up as a man, with little to be afraid of in this world.

"Yes, I'm sure. They said the farm doesn't use scarecrows, and there is a *fucking scarecrow standing on the hill!* Watching me!"

I heard a loud sigh on the other end.

"Are you saying you don't *believe* me?"

"I didn't *say* anything," he said, calmly.

"You sighed."

"Okay. Sorry. It's just... this sounds really..." He trailed off. "Nevermind."

"Please, just come over here. I'll explain everything."

"Why don't you come over here?"

"Because if I go outside, the scarecrow will get me!"

Silence. And then I realized, that sentence did sound pretty unhinged, on its own. "Listen, there's been really weird stuff happening on this farm." And then I launched into an explanation of everything: the list of rules, the sunflowers, the cornfield, even the pig man.

"Why didn't you tell me all this earlier?" he asked, when I'd finished.

"Because you wouldn't believe me. You still don't."

"I'm trying to. Just, this sounds like a lot of ghost story type stuff, you know?" Another sigh. "But look, I can tell you're upset. I'm coming over, okay? I'm leaving right now. Be there in a half hour."

I ended the call and stared at the curtains. For a minute, I was tempted to part them, to make sure the scarecrow hadn't gotten closer; but I wasn't going to disobey the rules.

When Derek arrived, I took every precaution to get him inside safely. I told him to park as close to the house as possible, look around for scarecrows, and then run as fast as he could.

As soon as he was inside safely, my fear melted away. We put on a movie, had some good laughs, and then went to bed.

But around 2 AM, something woke me with a start.

And when I sat up, I realized the bed was empty.

"Derek?" I called out, walking into the hallway. "Where are you?" When he didn't reply, I walked downstairs.

I found him standing in front of the window, peering outside. "Hey!" I hissed. "You're not supposed to look outside!"

"Sssshhh. There's someone out there."

My blood ran cold. I joined him at the window and scanned the fields. "I don't see anyone."

"No. There was definitely someone out there." His fingers inched towards his belt, and my heart plummeted when I saw the shiny black metal sticking out of his pocket.

"You brought your *gun?!*"

"You said you were scared!" he whispered back. "You said someone was out there! I didn't really believe you, but now I do. Aren't you glad I brought it?"

"No. I never want to be near that thing."

"Okay. We can have some stupid debate about gun rights later. Right now, there's someone out there. And if we just go back to sleep, we might not wake up in the morning."

"Come on..."

"I'm just telling it like it is."

I crossed my arms and stared out into the fields with him. And then—just as I was about to turn away—I saw it.

A shadowy figure, walking along the edge of the sunflower field.

Derek didn't waste any time. He unbolted the door and swung it open. "Hey! *You!* Get off our property! I've got a gun!"

The figure stopped. Paused.

And then sidestepped into the sunflowers.

Before I could stop him, he ran out of the house. "Derek!" I shouted, but he didn't stop. I paused at the threshold—and then I sprinted out after him. "Come back!"

Fuck. He was running straight for the sunflower field.

"Don't go in there!"

He probably wouldn't have even stopped. But when he got to the border, I screamed bloody murder at him, and he stopped for just a moment. "You can't go in there," I panted, grabbing his arm. "The sunflowers..."

"Yeah, you told me, they're evil or watch you or something. I think I can handle myself." He gestured to his gun. "And if I don't scare this fucker, he's going to come back and rape or murder or do whatever he came here to do."

With that, he disappeared into the foliage.

I stood there, panting, at the border of the field. *He'll be okay,* I lied to myself. *He'll be okay.* As the adrenaline faded, I lifted my head and scanned the flowers. They were all turned towards me, yellow petals appearing silver in the light of the full moon. *Okay. It's okay. They're all pointing the same direction. See?*—

Wait.

There was a single flower, in the center of the field, turned away from me.

My blood ran cold. "Come out of there!"

Silence. No pounding footsteps, no rustling, nothing. A chill ran over my body. "Please, come out," I begged, staring into the shadowy darkness under the flowers.

And then I heard it.

"HELP!"

His voice. Strangled, in pain.

I reacted instinctively. My feet hit the dirt and I stumbled into the darkness. Leaves brushed my body, scratched at my arms. "Derek?" I called.

The sunflowers stretched up, six or seven feet tall, their moonlit heads swaying in the breeze above me. I turned a full circle—looking in every direction for him—but all I saw were more stems, more leaves, more inky black shadows.

"Where are you?"

I stopped walking and listened. Straining my ears for any sort of sound. And then, after several seconds, I heard something—a soft rustling.

There was just one problem.

It was coming from right above my head.

I looked up. The sunflower directly above me was tilted straight down.

And this close, I saw it clearly. Its head wasn't full of seeds—no, where the seeds should have been, there was just an abyss of pure black. And there were things between the petals and the abyss—white, sharp things, all pointed towards the center—

Teeth.

I broke into a sprint. With both arms I pushed the sunflowers out of the way, forcing myself through the field. "*Derek!*" I screamed—but all I heard was more rustling above my head. As all the sunflowers tilted towards me. As their mouths opened and rows and rows of sharp fangs, gleaming in the moonlight, descended towards me.

Then something grabbed my arm.

I was dragged through the fields, the foliage snapping and rustling underneath me. "Help!" I screamed—but as my legs kicked against the dirt, I realized I was powerless, as I was dragged to my death—

I was staring up at the stars.

I shot up. The thing clasped around my arm wasn't a sunflower—it was a hand. An old, wrinkled hand. I looked up to see a bowler hat and a dark suit.

The old man from the farmstand.

And there, several feet away from me in the dirt, was Derek. He was breathing hard—*alive*—but his right arm was covered in dark blood that spilled out into the soil.

"I think it's time we had a talk," he said calmly, as he let go of my arm.

"What were you thinking, going into the sunflowers?" the old man asked, as he wound gauze around Derek's arm.

"What were *you* thinking? I saw you go into the field, too," he replied.

"I went *behind* the field. To hide from the crazy man with a gun."

"You were lurking around out there at 2 AM! What was I supposed to think?" Derek shot back, grimacing in pain.

"And you," the old man said, pointing squarely at me. "*You* should've known that if he couldn't kill whatever was attacking him with a gun, going in after him was an idiot move."

"I just—I wanted to save him," I said, arms crossed.

"Oh, so you were armed, too?"

"... No."

He shook his head. I caught the phrase *stupid kids* muttered under his breath. Then he took off his hat, set it in the middle of the table, and glanced at each of us. "I'm going to tell you what's going on here. And then, I hope, you can help me."

Derek and I exchanged a glance. "How do we know we can trust you?" he asked.

"He just saved our lives," I replied.

"He was hanging around outside in the middle of the night, for no good reason."

"It *was* a good reason," the old man snapped, glaring at Derek, "and if you just listened to me for a damn minute, you'd understand."

"Come on," I whispered, squeezing Derek's hand.

"Okay, fine."

The old man straightened himself, and then began to speak. "The Gershons started this farm almost 20 years ago. They bought the plot of land from an old widow, who had lived here her entire life. She didn't want to sell it, but she needed the money. Well, they drew up the contract—but at the last moment, they changed the paperwork and tricked her into selling it for half the price. When she realized she'd been tricked, she cursed the land itself. But they just laughed. They didn't believe in curses, or superstitions, or the supernatural." The old man stopped and looked pointedly at Derek. He broke eye contact and looked at the floor.

"Of course, as soon as they planted the sunflower field, they realized the curse was very real. Eventually, they tried to sell the property—but by that time, news of the curse had spread, and they would only get a fraction of what they paid. They weren't willing to lose their money, so they kept it. And with time, they learned that if they followed certain rules and stayed careful—they could grow some crops and turn a profit.

"But no one is perfect. After some close calls, the Gershons decided they didn't want to risk their lives—but were perfectly fine with risking other people's lives. So they started hiring people to tend to the farm. They preyed on the weak—the disadvantaged—the desperate. Single mothers. Undocumented immigrants. People who were new to the town, who hadn't yet heard of the curse—or were too desperate to care. The deal was a good one, too: a share of the crops, a place to live, and decent pay.

"This is where I come in. My daughter... was one of these people. She was a single mother. And I... I was terrible." He paused and swallowed, as if swallowing emotion. But his face remained stoic. "I wouldn't let her and her son stay with me when she was evicted from her apartment. I thought it would cause too much conflict with my wife, and I was trying so hard to make it work... but now I see that none of that mattered." He sucked in a breath. "A few weeks later, she was hired by the Gershons—and neither she nor my grandson were ever seen again."

Derek and I sat there in stunned silence. "I'm so sorry," I finally choked out. "That's... that's horrible."

"Then help me get them back," he said, a pleading look in his eye.

"Get them back?"

"They're not dead. You see... I recognize the voice in the cornfield. It's the voice of my grandson."

Silence fell over the three of us. Derek and I looked at each other. The old man must have noticed our confusion, because he continued: "The victims aren't always killed. Sometimes they're... transformed. Like my daughter and grandson, in the cornfield. Or the scarecrow. Or the pigs."

I clapped my hands over my mouth. "The pigs?!"

He nodded.

"No no no. I called the police. When I saw one. And they... they came and I think they..." Tears burned my eyes. "I think they killed him."

"I'm so sorry to hear that. But it's not your fault. The Gershons have a lot of power in this town. They have a deal with the police. Dirty cops have been known to get rid of evidence in the sunflower field." He sighed. "I've devoted the past three years of my life to this. I've run into every obstacle, know everything there is to know. A lot of it I learned from the widow's children directly."

"So is there a way to get them back? The people who were... transformed?" I asked.

"Yes. I was never able to get into the house before—the Gershons made sure of that. But now..." He reached into his pocket and pulled out what appeared to be a small mesh bag. Within, among what looked like dried plant material, I could make out something long and white—a bone? "This is what the widow used to create the curse. Her daughter told me it was hidden behind the medicine cabinet in the bathroom, and there it was. Using this, I should be able to reverse the curse's effects." He glanced at Derek, and then back at me. "So, will you help me?"

I paused, looking into the old man's blue eyes.

And then I nodded.

We began at dawn.

The sun crested over the hill, sending long shadows over the path. The old man led us to the edge of the cornfield, which now in the daylight, didn't look so ominous. The stalks swayed gently in the breeze, illuminated in gold from the rising sun.

"Are you ready?" he asked.

Derek and I stood several feet away as he lifted the

bag. He recited several sentences of Latin or some other language—something he'd memorized in his research, I assumed. He nearly shouted the last sentence. Then he dumped the contents of the bag on the ground.

The dried leaves scattered in the wind. The bone twirled in the air, then bounced into the dirt.

For a minute, nothing happened. But then I heard it: a soft rustling from within the corn. Slowly, it grew louder and louder. I grabbed Derek's hand and squeezed it, bracing myself for some eldritch horror to come out—

But it'd worked.

A woman walked out of the corn, tall and thin. Holding hands with a smiling little boy.

I watched, my eyes welling up with tears, as the woman hugged her father. Then as both of them hugged the little boy. "Come on," the old man said, wiping his eyes. "It's time for you to come home."

The old man started down the driveway, towards the main road, with his daughter and his grandson in his wake.

Dread twisted my gut. Something felt... off. He was just leaving? Without looking for the others? Without even a glance in our direction? I scanned the farm. But I didn't see anyone emerging, didn't hear any voices.

"Hey!" I called out. "What about the others?"

The old man stopped and turned around. He wasn't smiling. "I'm sorry," he said.

My heart sunk further. "What do you mean, you're sorry?"

"The curse can't be reversed," he said, his blue eyes

glinting in the rising sun. "The only way to free someone from the farm... is to give someone in their place."

No.

No. He doesn't mean—

"I'm sorry," the old man said. He put his arm around his daughter. She looked back at us with sadness in her eyes, holding her little boy's hand.

And then he continued down the driveway.

"*Don't walk away!*" I screamed.

"Emily..." Derek started.

"Come back here! *Right now!*"

"Emily!"

This time, Derek's voice had an odd quality to it. It was muffled, raspy. I whipped around—and froze.

Straw was poking out of Derek's mouth.

"No!" I screamed, stumbling over to him. But it was too late. His skin was sickly gray. His eyes were glassy and blank. And his lips... they almost looked like they'd been drawn on with marker.

I watched in horror as the man I loved turned into a scarecrow. "Derek," I sobbed. "Please..."

His body was still above me. Arms stretched stiffly out at his sides. Flannel shirt stuffed with straw. Burlap head hanging limply on his shoulders.

And then he moved.

His head swung wildly towards me. His eyes—now nothing more than buttons—fixed squarely on me.

I ran. I ran as fast as I could towards the house. But I could feel something changing inside me; everything felt off-balance. My legs felt all wrong, bending and twisting underneath me. I stumbled inside and collapsed to the floor, crying.

But I knew.

I knew I was changing, too.

For some reason, my changes are happening more slowly than Derek's. But when I look in the mirror, I can see the changes: my nose is longer. My ears are twisted. My skin is pinker.

So I tried to type this up as quickly as I could. Please, stay far away from Gershon Farm. Don't buy their stuff, don't go to work there, don't do anything. Run as fast as you can and never look back.

I would say more, but it's getting harder to type. The space between my fingers is melting away. My hands are growing stiff. In just an hour or so, they will be hooves—and I will have no way of communicating with the outside world.

So please.

Whatever you do, don't come to Gershon Farm.

MY NEIGHBOR GOT A DOG. I DON'T THINK IT'S A DOG

My neighbor Jack adopted a border collie two weeks ago. At least, that's what I thought. Now I'm not so sure.

I first saw Toto out on a walk. He was sniffing some of the flowers growing next to the sidewalk as Jack waited, scrolling through his cell phone. "Wow! You got a dog!" I called out, waving.

"I certainly did! His name's Toto. Border collie mix."

Toto stopped sniffing the flowers and glanced up at me. I'd encountered many dogs on this street, and they ran the whole gamut of dog greetings: from curious sniffs to protective growling to jumping up and licking my face.

None of them just... stared... at me like Toto did.

"Wow, he's beautiful! And so big for a collie mix!" I began to crouch down. "Can I pet him?"

"Oh--actually he's a little shy," Jack said. "Having a little trouble adapting, you know? But I'm sure he'll warm up in a few days." He tugged gently on the leash. "C'mon, Toto."

I watched as they walked away from me.

The next time I saw Toto, I was dropping something off for Jack. He'd lent me his drill for a home improvement project and I'd never returned it.

But when I rang the doorbell, I didn't hear the usual barking I did with other dog owners. Instead--just the *pat-pat-pat* of feet against wood.

And then Toto's face was in the glass inset of the door, staring out at me. Not barking or growling or pawing at the door. Just... staring.

Before I could think anything of it, Jack's footsteps sounded through the hall, and the door swung open. "Hey, Amir!"

"Just wanted to give this back."

"Oh, thanks! Hey, why don't you come in? I'm just about to pull some cookies out of the oven."

Jack was an avid baker, and I couldn't say no to his cookies. I stepped inside and followed the warm cinnamon smell to the kitchen. Toto followed behind me.

But I could tell something was... off.

I don't have a dog, but I have a lot of friends with dogs. And we can always tell the dog is coming our way when we hear that mistakable *clicking* sound of his or her nails against the floor. It was instinctual at this point—hear that sound and scarf down the last bit of steak, or put the chocolate out of reach, or get ready to get licked on the face.

This dog... didn't make that sound.

No clicking of nails against the wooden floor. Just... sort of a dull *thump, thump, thump* with each step.

I glanced back at Toto. And I realized his movements were a little odd, too. His steps were a little jerky, a little stiff, a little clumsy for a dog of his build. He wasn't limping or anything—just, overall, the movements didn't look quite right.

"Hope you like snickerdoodles," Jack said, pulling the tray out of the oven.

"Wow. They look *amazing.*"

"My Nana's recipe," he said proudly. "Ate these every day after school. Fond memories."

I picked up a cookie and took a bite.

But I had an audience. Toto was staring at me.

Well, that wasn't weird. Dogs loved to stare at

people food. I was just about to ask Jack if these cookies were safe for dogs—but his phone went off. "Oh, sorry man, gotta take this," he muttered as he disappeared down the hall and into the office.

I sat down at the kitchen table. Toto didn't move—just stared at me from across the kitchen. Weirdly, he wasn't licking his lips or anything as he stared hungrily at the cookie in my hand.

"You're a weird dog. But I like you," I said.

The dog continued to stare.

"I'm sorry I can't give you any cookies. I don't know if they're safe."

More staring.

"You're going to like it here. It's a good neighborhood."

He canted his head.

And as he did… I realized there was something off. Something about the way the light bounced off his fur. It was a little too shiny, a little too well groomed, for a rough-and-tumble collie dog. I squinted at him, studying him—

And then I heard something.

A quiet, rushing sound. Like a whisper. And I guess I must've been imagining it, but it almost sounded like… God, it almost sounded like someone whispering.

"*Help me.*"

I stared at the dog—

"Sorry about that!" Jack said, wandering back in. "I just had to take that, it was a new client, and we're trying to keep him… how do you like the cookies?"

"They were amazing," I said, standing up. "But I've

got to go. Mandy and the girls will be back from softball anytime now, and I'm supposed to have dinner ready."

"Oh, dinner duty, huh?" He motioned at the snickerdoodles. "Take some back with you. Say you made 'em from scratch."

"Mandy knows I can't bake like that. But thanks."

I stepped out the front door, waving back at Jack and Toto. Jack waved, grinning. The dog just stared at me, as usual.

But this time, his black, glassy eyes sent chills down my spine.

"I swear. There's something fucked up about that dog."

The girls were asleep, and Mandy and I were enjoying some much-needed quality time. We sat on the couch with a bottle of wine, an episode of The Office in the background as we talked about our days.

Mandy was surprisingly interested in the story. "So you've never heard him bark?"

"No."

"And he walks weird? And just... stares at you?"

"Yup."

She shook her head, laughing. "That does sound really weird. Even weirder than Aunt Polly's dog. Remember her?"

"Is that the one that makes the weird screeching sound?"

"Yeah."

We laughed about it, hung out some more, and then

eventually went to sleep. But even an hour after Mandy had fallen asleep, around midnight, I was lying wide awake. Thinking about that fucking dog.

And then I decided to do something really stupid.

I probably never would have done it, if I hadn't drunk three glasses of wine. But with liquid courage, I crept downstairs—and slipped out of the house.

The lights were still on in Jack's house. When I got there, I ducked behind his hydrangea and peered into the window.

Golden light spilled into the living room from the kitchen. Jack was sitting on the couch, looking at his laptop. Toto was lying on the floor, his black eyes glittering in the low light. Surprisingly, he didn't seem to detect my presence at all.

After several minutes, Jack shut the laptop and disappeared down the hallway. Toto watched him, but didn't follow.

I was about to go back home—

And then I saw it.

Toto stood up. And then, using the couch to balance himself, he stood up again.

He was standing on two legs.

I watched with wide eyes as he walked into the kitchen. Stood in front of the refrigerator. And then—a small opening appeared, smack-dab in the middle of Toto's chest.

A human hand came out.

It grasped the refrigerator door, pulled it open. Greedily grabbed some food off the shelf. Then the 'dog' sat back down on the floor, cross-legged, and the hand

—holding a leftover sandwich—disappeared into the hole.

I stared through the window, my heart pounding in my chest.

It's a costume.

There's a... person... in there.

I hightailed it out of there. Wrapped myself in blankets and lay next to my wife, wide awake, thoughts rolling through my head.

I didn't expect to fall asleep. But I must have, because the next thing I knew, a loud noise woke me from a deep sleep.

Knocking.

Someone was knocking on my front door.

Bleary-eyed, I hobbled down the stairs. I looked through the peephole—and saw Jack. Standing on my front porch.

Looking incredibly angry.

I don't know what he wants. But I think he knows that I know. That for some reason, he's keeping what appears to be a full-grown man in his house, wearing a dog costume and pretending to be a dog.

Because when I went over there that night, still tipsy from the wine... I totally forgot he has security cameras.

I decided to ignore Jack. Since I knew he was keeping a man in his house dressed as a dog, I figured that was my safest bet. Besides, it was almost 2 AM. He'd just assume I was asleep, right?

"I know you're in there, Amir! Open up!"

He sounded angry. *Really* angry. I shrunk against the door, holding my breath, trying not to make a sound.

"Amir!"

He knocked for a few more minutes. Then, finally, I heard his footsteps retreat off the porch.

I stood there for several more minutes, in case he came back. Then I checked all the locks and crept back upstairs.

For the rest of the night I tossed and turned, trying to figure out what to do. *I should just call the police. But what if it's... consensual? What if that man, for whatever reason, agreed to pretend to be Jack's dog? Does he self-identify as a dog? Is it a furry thing?*

But then I thought of how *angry* Jack sounded.

And when dawn broke, I called the cops.

They didn't believe me at first. But, finally, they agreed to go over to Jack's and check it out. I ran over to the living room window and parted the blinds, staring out across the street at Jack's house.

By the time the police car pulled up, I could hear Mandy's steps above me. But I remained glued to the window. Watching.

Two officers, a tall woman and a plump man, exited the vehicle and stepped up onto the porch. I saw the woman raise her fist and knock. I waited, holding my breath. But as the door cracked open, I heard it, clear as day.

Barking.

Jack began talking to the officers, his expression darkening. And then a blur of brown-and-white fur shot out.

My jaw dropped as the dog leapt up onto the officers. A pink tongue shot out and it began licking them, letting out happy yelps.

No.

It was a real dog.

It had to be. It was considerably smaller than the two officers—no way an adult man could fit in there. And it was barking, and licking, and jumping around. The dog suit I'd seen yesterday hadn't even been able to open its mouth.

"What are you doing?"

I turned around to see Mandy there, staring at me.

"Oh, uh..."

I sat down and explained everything to her that happened last night. But I could tell, she didn't believe me. I couldn't really blame her—after all, she could see a very live, very real dog jumping around Jack and the police officers.

"So you're saying you think... in the middle of the night... he let the dog-man go and adopted a real one?!"

"I know it sounds crazy but—"

"It does sound crazy! And you shouldn't go calling the cops on our neighbors, unless something *really* bad is happening. If our house is on fire, or if someone breaks in, you think Jack is gonna want to help us?"

"But—I saw it. It was a *person*. I swear."

"You were drunk. You probably just saw the dog

jumping up while Jack was behind him or something, so it looked like a hand sticking out."

"Mandy, I swear—"

She shook her head and walked out of the room.

Soon after, the officers came by and confirmed it. Jack was in possession of a large, very friendly, 100% real collie dog.

"That son of a bitch," I whispered, staring out the window as they pulled away.

I knew the truth. Even if everyone else thought I was crazy, I know what I saw. That's why, later that night—when I saw Jack's car pull out—I snuck out of the house and crept into his backyard. Now that I remembered the security cameras, I was careful to forge a path that avoided them.

But as soon as I stepped up onto the deck—

Arf! Arf! Arf!

The collie was scratching at the back door, barking at me.

"Ssssshhh!" I tried the door. Locked, of course. Swearing, I made my way around to the side door. It was locked too. *I'll have to try tomorrow. Maybe I can come over for more cookies. I asked the police to keep my name out of the whole thing... maybe he isn't certain it was me.* I shook my head. *Yeah, right. Of course he knows it was me.*

I started towards the front of the house—

Thump!

I turned around. A rattling, metallic sound, and then —*thump!*

It was coming from the basement.

I ran over to the bilco doors. They were locked—but with a padlock. Thankfully, I had a pair of bolt cutters in my garage. I crept back home, grabbed the bolt cutters, and made my way back into the yard. With a swift downward motion—*SNAP!*—the door was unlocked.

I lifted the door open.

Two black, glinting eyes stared back at me.

It was him. The man in the dog suit, sitting in the center of the basement. A collar wrapped around his neck, the chain fastened to one of the support holes.

I grabbed the bolt cutters and ran down the stairs. "I'm going to get you out of here," I whispered, rushing towards him.

No reaction. He just stared at me, still as a statue, his plastic dog fur shining in the light from the one bare bulb on the ceiling.

A chill crept over me. Why wasn't he... reacting more? He didn't have to act like a dog anymore. Jack wasn't around. Why wasn't he calling for help? Or thanking me? Or something?

Why was he just... staring at me... through the dog suit?

I crouched on the cold cement floor, positioning the bolt cutters across the chain. "I'm going to set you free. Hold still—"

Ziiiip.

A hand shot out of the dog's chest—and grabbed me by the arm.

"Hey!"

But the hand only tightened. I tried to tug free—but the nails dug into my skin. "Let me go!" I shouted, but the hand was pulling me in. Towards the dog's lifeless, glassy eyes—the plastic nose—the painted mouth—

And then I heard something.

A whisper.

"Behind you."

I whipped around. And my blood ran cold.

A silhouette sat perched above the basement's doors, peering down at us. *Jack.* I grabbed the bolt cutters and squeezed.

SNAP.

The chain broke in two. The dog-man leapt up and, with amazing speed for wearing a heavy costume, bounded up the stairs towards Jack. But Jack was too fast—before he could slip past, he grabbed the dog by the arms and pushed him back down the stairs.

Thump, thump, thump.

He was still at the bottom.

I grabbed the bolt cutters and ran up the steps. In one quick motion, I swung them at Jack. He ducked.

"You don't know what you're doing, Amir. You don't know the whole story."

"You're keeping a guy locked in your basement and forcing him to wear a dog costume!" I raised the bolt cutters again—

"Amir, just *listen* to me! He's not who you think he—"

THWACK.

They hit the side of his head.

Not that hard. I wasn't swinging to kill. But Jack crumpled to the ground, clutching his head, groaning in pain. And in that moment, I bounded down the stairs and grabbed one of the dog-man's paws. "Here, come on, quick," I whispered, pulling at the fake paw.

Slowly, he rose.

One human hand popped out of his chest. Then a second. I helped him undo the clasps on the belly, and under the arms; then, the costume slowly crumpled away from him. Then I was staring at an adult man, taller than myself, wearing a border collie mask.

But he didn't reach up to pop off the mask.

No. He just stood there, absolutely still. Staring down at me with those lifeless, glassy dog eyes. Plastic brown fur shining in the light.

Something about this felt... *wrong*.

I backed away. Backed up the steps and out onto the lawn. His eyes never left mine; he turned his head, slowly, to watch me go.

And then—when I'd gotten about ten feet from the basement door—he bolted up the steps and ran across the lawn, for the woods.

But when he got to the treeline, he stopped.

He turned around. Slowly pulled off the mask. And then he was staring at me, grinning with a smile of yellowed, rotten teeth.

"Thank you," he whispered.

And then he disappeared into the darkness.

But I couldn't move. Couldn't breathe. Because I recognized that face. I'd seen it on the news... a man who'd been convicted of stalking and murdering three women. Who then escaped from prison, earlier this year.

And the pieces clicked into place.

His name... if I remembered correctly, it was Sam Baker... and Jack, he was Jack Baker.

Jack slowly pulled himself up, groaning in pain. "Amir..." he said, staring into my eyes. "Did you just set my brother free?"

I USED CHATGPT AND I REGRET EVERYTHING

I'm an indie horror author. And when I say "indie," that's really just a cool way of saying "unknown." I write short horror anthologies and self-publish them on Amazon. It's a good thing I have a real day job, because there's no way in hell I could support myself on writing alone.

Anyway.

For the past several months, I've been brainstorming ways to increase my revenue. And suddenly, in the middle of the night, it came to me. *Artificial Intelligence.* I could make Chat-GPT, or whatever was the up-and-coming AI, write stories for me. Then I could slap them all in a book, say I wrote them, and viola! Instant cash.

My first prompt was pretty vague.

Write a horror story.

Chat-GPT spit out something pretty generic—but it was actually better than I expected it to be.

On a dark and stormy night, Sarah was sitting home alone. Suddenly, she heard a knock at the door. She opened it to find a man standing on the porch. Something about him looked off, and she realized it was because he was smiling too wide.

I won't bore you with the whole story, but basically the man came inside the house, the lights went out in a conveniently-timed blackout, and then he killed her.

Not good enough, but... also not terrible. So I decided to try again, and be a little more specific with my prompt.

Write a horror story about a doppelganger.

On a dark and stormy night, a young woman named Emily was watching TV home alone. She heard a footstep outside the window. When she looked up, she saw a woman looking in the window. However, the woman looked just like her, except for the bloody gash on her head.

I read on... and began to smile.

It wasn't just good. It was *great.* Heart-racing scenes of the doppelganger stalking her through the house, a final twist where the injured doppelganger was actually coming to warn the main character about her impending death...

It was a lot better than anything I'd written recently.

I brought the story over to a new Word document and edited it up. Then I posted it to all my social media pages—and it *blew up.*

Jackpot.

I got two thousand new followers. My sales went

through the roof. Amazon gave my book the little orange *#1 Best Seller in Horror Anthologies* tag.

That night, with a glass of wine in hand, I ran back over to Chat-GPT. Opened my ideas document—some of which had been languishing there for years—and began rapid-fire copy-pasting them into the AI. Any story that was halfway decent went right into the queue.

But then... things started to get a little... weird. I entered the prompt:

Write a horror story about a creepy monster who lives in the basement.

Hannah had always been afraid of the basement. It was always dark down there and there were lots of cobwebs. She always let Mommy or Daddy go into the basement for her.

But one night her parents were out. She was too scared to ask her babysitter, so when her rainbow ball rolled down the steps, she decided to go down there herself.

I stopped.

I had a rainbow ball, as a little girl. It was one of my favorite toys. And there was one night that it rolled into the basement. Nothing happened; there wasn't a monster down there. But it was still a creepy experience that I vividly remember, 20 years later.

Just a coincidence, I told myself, taking a long sip of wine. *I've generated like fifty stories at this point... there are bound to be some weird coincidences.*

But still. ChatGPT seemed to always go the vague

route. Why would it say a "rainbow" ball? That seemed like an oddly-specific detail.

I shook my head and entered the next prompt.

Write a horror story about someone who sees something terrifying on their Ring camera.

Johnny installed a Ring camera next to his doorbell for his own safety and security. One night, he was woken up at 3:24 AM by a notification on his phone. When he opened the camera feed, he saw an old woman in a white dress standing in his front yard, standing next to the old well.

I had an old well in my front yard.

One of those little stone ones with a peaked roof. The house was old, and it had been here when I bought it, even though the well itself had been filled in long ago.

I continued reading, but no other details matched my house. I let out a sigh of relief, then entered the next prompt.

Write a horror story about a woman who is visited by a vengeful spirit.

But the words ChatGPT spit out made my blood run cold.

On a dark and stormy night, Blair was home alone, reading a book.

It used my name. Blair.

In all the other stories, it used very common, generic first names. *Sarah. Emily. Johnny.* I held my breath as the words popped up, one-by-one, on my screen.

She was starting to get sleepy, but then she heard a

noise coming from her front porch. She strained her ears, listening for a knock, but none came.

I picked up the glass of wine, my hands beginning to shake. I took a sip—

Thump.

"Must... must just be the wind," I whispered to myself. The next sentence popped up on the screen:

Blair thought it was the wind, but it wasn't.

The glass fell out of my hand. It shattered to a million pieces, and dark wine oozed across the linoleum like blood.

Fuck.

I grabbed a towel from the kitchen and began to sop up the mess. *Just another coincidence. That's what all the horror stories say, when there's a weird sound. Must be the wind. Must be the house settling. Etc., etc.*

If it were *just* that, maybe I could persuade myself. But the rainbow ball. The old well. And using my name...

I looked up from cleaning, my throat dry, and read the next paragraph.

As Blair cleaned up the wine she'd spilled, she heard the sound again. Louder this time.

Oh, no, no—

THUMP!

I jumped. My hands shook as I held the wet rag in my hands. "H-hello?" I called out, my voice echoing in the empty house.

No answer.

I jumped up and ran over to every door, making sure

they were all locked. Then I checked the windows. Panting, I ran back to the computer.

Blair made sure all the doors were locked—but it was too late.

I stared at the screen, my heart pounding.

It was already inside the house.

All the blood drained out of my face. I grabbed the computer and ran down the hallway, locking myself in my bedroom. Then I dragged my dresser across the carpet, in front of the door.

THUMP!

It sounded like it was *right outside my door.*

I backed away from the door. Until my back was pressed against the window. Then I turned towards the cold glass—and saw something that made my blood run cold.

There was an old woman, wearing a white tattered dress, standing next to the well.

And then she began to walk towards me. I gripped the windowsill, my knuckles white, wishing this were a two-story house. But in a few minutes, she'd be at the window, with only this thin pane of glass between us.

She continued towards me in strange, halting movements. As if she didn't know quite how to walk. As if... she was trying to imitate everything she'd observed about human movement.

Imitating... like an AI.

THUMP!

The door shook. A shadow appeared in the crack underneath. *No, no, no—*

Tap-tap-tap.

I whipped around—to see a woman with her face pressed up against the window. Not the old woman. A woman who looked just like *me,* with a bloody gash on her forehead.

Warning me of my own death. Like in the story.

The door shook again, and I pictured the man with the too-wide smile outside.

"I'm sorry," I sobbed. "I'm so sorry."

THUMP!

Tap-tap-tap.

Shuffle-shuffle.

In a last, frantic attempt to save my life, I grabbed the computer—and closed out of ChatGPT.

And just like that, the noise stopped.

I crouched down and peered at the crack underneath the door. No shadow. I ran over to the window. Nothing. Leaves swayed slightly in the breeze. Water glinted off the grass.

I collapsed onto the bed and began to sob. I didn't fall asleep until dawn broke—and the first rays of sunlight illuminated the only trace they left behind: a smudge of dark blood on the glass.

So I'm begging you. Please, please don't use any artificial intelligence, like ChatGPT, to write your stories for you.

Or you might end up like me.

MY MILKSHAKE BRINGS SOMETHING TERRIBLE TO THE YARD

I grab the blender out from the cabinet. Plop it onto the counter. Plug it in. Stare at its curved blades, shining in the low light.

Then I swing open the freezer door. Grab the half-eaten tub of chocolate ice cream. Reach into the fridge, grab the carton of skim milk.

3 scoops of ice cream. 2 cups of milk. 1 deep breath.

My hands shake in the air, over the 'ON' button.

Then I close my eyes and push.

The whirring sound fills my ears. But even though I can't hear it, I know it's coming. The hairs on the back of my neck prickle. But I don't turn around.

I just close my eyes and wait for it all to be over.

It all started five years ago.

We'd listened to the song "Milkshake" by Kelis

about twenty times while doing each other's makeup, dancing around, and talking about boys. We were seventeen, without a care in the world... except the party happening later that night at Matt's house.

"Hey. I have an idea." Irena, our resident goth girl, turned down the music and smiled to us with a sparkle in her eye. Her black hair nearly reached her waist, and she was wearing so much eyeshadow it looked like her eyes were just floating in their sockets. "For us to look *really* hot tonight."

"Yeah? What's that?" Carmen asked, not looking up from the mirror.

"Just a little thing I found," she said with a giggle. "Leave everything to me."

We should've realized Irena was going to pull some witchcraft shit. Especially when she lit a few of my candles and started muttering to herself. But we were barely paying attention. Carmen was dusting an extra layer of glowy foundation over her perfectly brown skin, and I was running a straightener over a stubborn curl of hair.

Her chants melted into the repetitive chorus of the song:

My milkshake brings all the boys to the yard...

"Landon won't even talk to me."

Irena found me sitting in the corner, drinking some peppermint schnapps, glaring at the well-built football player across the room. Everyone was laughing and having the time of their lives, while I couldn't take my eyes off the guy I'd pined over all year. Talking to another girl.

A blonde, because of course. I frowned at my own dark hair—and the curl that ran down my shoulder, springing back to life on this humid South Carolina night.

"I think I know just the thing to cheer you up," Irena said, taking my hand. "Come on."

She led me into the kitchen. My confusion only grew when she opened up Matt's freezer and pulled out a massive tub of Cookies 'n' Cream ice cream. Then she grabbed a cup, a spoon, and a carton of milk.

"Have a milkshake."

"No way. I've had way too many calories today already."

"Seriously," she said. "Just make one. I promise it'll make you feel better."

I sighed. Cookies 'n' Cream *was* one of my favorite flavors. Finally, I reached for the spoon. Plunged it into the ice cream. *Plop.* Grabbed the milk and poured it in. *Glug-glug-glug.*

Then I grabbed the spoon—and began to stir.

As soon as I began to stir... something happened. I could feel a shift in the air. The humidity evaporating. The loud sounds of conversation and music seemed to grow quieter. The light overhead flickered, for just a second.

I paused, looking up at the light. "What was—"
Thump.

I glanced up to see Landon standing in the doorway.

Staring right at me.

At first, my heart fluttered. But then my butterflies turned to dread. He was just... *staring*... at me. Not even blinking. Not even moving.

"... Landon?" I asked, hesitantly.

I glanced at Irene. She was grinning.

"Landon?"

His mouth, slowly, stretched into a grin.

But the grin didn't reach his eyes, which remained laser-focused on me.

"Landon! There you are!" The blonde came rushing into the room. Then she glanced at me. "What are you doing? I thought we were gonna—"

He turned his head. Still grinning.

Then he raised his arms—

And in one swift motion, bashed her head into the floor.

Screams erupted. A pool of blood seeped into the kitchen tile. But all I could do was stare at Landon—who was now walking right towards me.

"Get away from me!" I shouted, backing up.

He quickened his pace, reaching for my arm.

I darted away from him. Ran out the back door, into the yard. Ran around the side of the house and sprinted out onto the sidewalk—

I froze.

Several men stood on the sidewalk. Motionless in the darkness, little more than silhouettes. Front doors of the surrounding houses stood wide open. The men varied in age, from middle-aged fathers to teenagers like me.

Thump-thump-thump—

I whipped around. Landon was closing in on me, jogging at full speed. Hands flattened as they pierced the air, like sprinters' when they're going for the gold.

I turned and ran for the car.

I dove into the front seat just as Landon caught up with me. His face hit the window, hard—and then he began clawing at the door. I screamed. The shadows shifted and I realized the other men were catching up to me, too. *Thump*—a portly one rammed himself into the passenger door. Over and over. As if the blood trickling down his forehead didn't even register. An elderly man climbed up on the trunk, pounding at the back window. Another teenager joined Landon in trying to pry the door open—

"Shit. The keys."

I'd given them to Carmen. She was the only one with pockets. "Fuck you!" I screamed at Landon, whose wild eyes stared at me from the other side of the glass. "Get the fuck away from me!"

Oh, no.

One of the men—a nerdy man in his thirties—grabbed a large rock by the side of the driveway. I watched in horror as he lifted it over his head, aiming for my window—

Crash.

The rock flew through the back window. As soon as it fell away, four mens' hands thrust their way into the car, blindly groping the air.

I screamed, opened the door, and lunged out into the air. A hand grabbed mine—and I looked up into

Landon's crazed eyes. "No!" I screamed, jerking my hand back. And then I ran as fast as I could.

After twenty minutes, I found myself alone.

After what happened, Carmen lived her life never making milkshakes. I thought I'd do the same. It seemed a small price to pay.

But then it happened.

Last night, in my small town, a woman was raped. The cops think he's hiding somewhere, and while they don't have the means to flush every straight man out into the open, I do.

I'm not sure I'll survive. I've barricaded the doors and windows, but I think that somehow, they might find a way in. So I'm writing this up and posting it before they have the chance. As I sip my milkshake, I can see them beginning to swarm. Walking down the sidewalk, coming out of their houses, homing in on me.

But I know I'm doing the right thing. Because I've always wondered something: why the other guys at the party didn't follow me out. Why more men from the neighborhood didn't come out of their homes. And it became crystal clear when Landon was not only arrested for hurting the blonde girl, but forcing oral sex on a classmate.

Maybe the cops will arrest more than one man today.

I smile and take another sip.

THE SAME MAN IS APPEARING BEHIND MY FRIENDS ON ZOOM

"Hi, everyone."

It was our weekly D&D session. Greta, Johnny, Zach, and I had been best friends on campus, but our jobs put us all over the country. This D&D campaign, meeting up every Saturday afternoon on a video call, made us all feel a little closer. It was the highlight of my week.

But not this time.

Because about fifteen minutes in, motion caught my eye.

Behind Greta, out on the sidewalk, a man was walking by. People walked by all the time—her apartment window faced a busy street—but this man looked... different. He was wearing mostly black, and walked with a strange limp as he made his way past her window.

And something almost looked... familiar... about him?

I clicked on Greta's image, maximizing her video

feed. But he was too far away, and the resolution was too low to see his face. And then he was gone.

Weird.

"Allison? What did you roll?"

My attention snapped back to the game. "Uh, sorry. It's a 3."

As Greta described an epic failure, where my rogue's bow malfunctioned and hit her square in the face, I aimlessly stared at Zach's video feed. *He looks good.* We'd dated for a few months, way back when, but things didn't work out. *Maybe they could work out now?* But long distance... it would be difficult. Besides... I wasn't really ready for a relationship, right now. I was six months sober, trying to get my life on track, trying to forget the shitshow that was senior year.

And then another flash of motion caught my eye.

Behind Johnny.

Johnny was sitting at the local Starbucks, loudly slurping a caramel macchiato through his straw. Behind him people walked to and fro—a mother with a crying little girl, two teenage boys shoving each other and laughing.

But that wasn't what caught my eye.

Beyond them, in the parking lot—was a tall man dressed in black.

Huh. I clicked on Johnny's feed and leaned into the screen. Again, the resolution was too low to make out his face. But he seemed to be wearing the same bowler hat, the same long black jacket.

Has to be a coincidence. Greta lived down in Oklahoma—hundreds of miles away from Johnny. It couldn't be the same guy. There was no way.

"Roll for damage, Allison."

I grabbed the D20 off my desk. When I looked back at Johnny's screen—

The man was gone.

I shook my head. *Just a coincidence.* I sucked in a breath as the die clattered against the wood. "18," I said, looking back at the screen.

"Nice," Zach said, sarcastically.

My eyes snapped to his screen.

He was sitting in his usual spot: on the moldy-green couch in the living room. For a second I imagined myself sitting next to him. Snuggled up against his shoulder.

His face was in shadow now, as sunlight streamed through the gauzy curtains behind him. But I could still make out his bright blue eyes, the curves of his rugged jaw. Maybe I should take my chances. I know I had a lot of emotional baggage, a lot of things to work on. But maybe we could work on them *together*. Maybe—

I froze.

Movement. From behind the curtains.

A silhouette, walking by.

A silhouette with a limp.

My blood ran cold. *No, no, no. There's no way.* The shadow passed, disappearing beyond the edge of the window.

"Uh... guys?" I started, my voice wavering. "Did any of you see that? That... that guy, with the bowler hat and the limp?"

Greta's eyebrows furrowed.

And then she said something that froze every muscle in my body.

"You mean the guy that's standing right outside your window?"

I whipped around.

Then I ran over to the window. I thought I saw a flash of movement—a sweep of black—but only for an instant. Or was it my imagination? The grass rippled in the wind and the pine trees swayed, but the sidewalk, and the street, were empty.

"I—I saw him in each of your videos," I stuttered. "Wearing all black, right? With the hat and the long jacket and the—"

"I only saw him in your video," Greta replied. "You're saying you saw that guy... in *our* videos?"

I nodded.

But the confused mutters from the other players told me they hadn't seen him. Only Greta had seen him walking by, behind *me*. I bit my lip, my hands frozen on the keyboard.

"Weird coincidence," Zach said finally. "But a lot of people wear black coats, and a lot of bald guys wear hats."

"But he was limping, too."

"Glitch in the matrix kinda thing, then?" Zach replied, shrugging. "I don't know. Can we resume playing, though?"

Greta started up again and I leaned back in my chair, sighing. I tried to forget about the man, though, and put all my focus on the game.

For almost an hour, everything went fine.

And then I saw it.

At the very edge of Greta's screen—just barely poking out from behind the window frame—was the man. All I could see was his sleeve, half of one of his legs, and a shiny black shoe.

How long has he been standing there?!

"Greta—he's right outside your window!" I nearly shouted.

Greta paused for a second. Then she got up, went over to the window, and peered out. "I don't see anyone," she said finally, sitting back down.

But the instant she sat back down, he stepped out into frame.

He limped out into view, onto the sidewalk. I still couldn't see his face—but I could tell that his head was turned, as if he were looking into Greta's window. He made his way down the sidewalk and disappeared—

And then stepped into Johnny's video.

His stride didn't even break. It was like he had just seemlessly *walked* from one video feed to the next. He walked down the sidewalk outside the Starbucks—his head still turned, as if staring in at Johnny. And then—

His shadow appeared behind the gauzy curtains at Zach's. He appeared to slow down, like he was taking his time, staring in at Zach through the translucent curtains. His halting, limping steps jerked his whole body as he made his way across.

Then he walked out of view.

And I knew it was my turn.

I jumped out of my chair and ran to the window. Half of me expected to see nothing; just an empty street and sidewalk. But no. It wasn't empty. In the darkening dusk, I could see the man, standing on the other side of the street. Eyes hidden in the shadows beneath his bowler hat.

My blood turned to ice. I stood there, frozen, at the window. We stared at each other for a few seconds, and then—

He lifted his hand and curled his index finger.

Beckoning me.

I backed away from the window. My legs trembled beneath me. There was no way this could even happen. Whoever that man was—he wasn't *real*—because there was no way he could instantly be in Oklahoma, then Ohio, then New York—

My legs hit the chair. I turned around, away from the window, back to my friends.

Except they weren't there.

Each video feed was malfunctioning. A jumble of pixelated shapes, lagging and jumping and twisting together. "Greta? Johnny? Zach?" I shouted. Only a distorted series of clicks answered me.

I turned back to the window—

The man was closer now. Standing in the middle of the street.

I wrenched the window open. "Hey! Get out of here!" I shouted, trying to hide the fear in my voice. "I'm calling the cops!"

I ran around the house, making sure every door was locked. Then I went up to my room and locked the door. Hid myself in the blankets and began to sob.

But I didn't call the cops.

Because I finally knew why he looked familiar.

Senior year. The party. The four of us piling in the car. *My* car. "I feel fine," I'd said, waving off any concerns about driving drunk.

But I *was* drunk.

Just not total blackout-drunk, like the other three.

I was the only one who'd seen the man walk out into the crosswalk. The tall man, dressed in black, which camouflaged him in the night. But I didn't see him soon enough. The brakes screeched underneath me, but it was too late.

A sickening *thump*.

The bowler hat went flying off into darkness.

"What—what was that?" Greta slurred from the backseat, as Zach puked and Johnny drifted in and out of sleep.

"N—nothing," I'd replied. Before gunning it and tearing out onto the highway.

I pull the blankets tighter around me and pray for him to leave. But even now, I can hear something above me. Coming from the attic. *Th-thump. Th-thump. Th-thump.*

The footsteps of a limping man.

I'm not sure I'll survive the night. I'm writing this so at least somebody knows what happened, if I don't make it.

I'm sorry.

23ANDME SAYS I HAVE A SECOND MOTHER

This summer, I decided to get my DNA sequenced by 23andme. I wanted to know my ancestry, as well as find out if I'm a carrier for any genetic disorders, since my husband and I want to try and get pregnant soon.

When the results came back, everything was what I expected. I was Romanian and German. I had the sun-sneeze reflex. Etc. The surprise came when I clicked on the "Relatives" tab. At the top of the list, it showed my parents.

Except, there weren't two parents.

There were *three*.

John T.
Father, 50.0% DNA shared
Agnes T.
Mother, 50.0% DNA shared
G
Mother, 50.0% DNA shared

I stared at the last one. *Uh... what?* I scrolled up and

down the list, but the rest looked normal. One of my brothers came up, along with an aunt and some cousins.

Curious, I clicked on G's profile. But there wasn't any other information. To see details, like her ancestry or shared relatives, I'd need to 'connect' with her.

Probably just a glitch or something. Or maybe my mom made two accounts by accident. I closed my laptop and tried to forget about it.

But for the rest of the day, it bothered me. Like a little itch in the back of my brain. *Maybe it isn't a duplicate account or a total glitch. Maybe she's some secret aunt or something, and 23andme just overestimated the shared DNA.* I'd read the horror stories, of 23andme uncovering family secrets like that.

So that evening, I decided to hit "Connect." I didn't really expect her to accept.

But just a few days later, she did.

I went over to the 23andme website, my heart pounding. When I scrolled down, I saw my ancestry composition and G's, side-by-side. Her ancestry looked like my mom's—almost 100% Romanian. But... it was slightly different.

My heart pounded faster. I opened three tabs: my mom's ancestry, my dad's, G's, and mine. My eyes darted between them, comparing them. Studying them. And after several minutes, I realized it.

I was 1% Scandinavian. But neither my mother nor my father had any Scandinavian ancestry.

Only "G" did.

A chill went down my spine. I stared at G's profile. At her empty profile picture.

Who is she?

I told my husband all about it. He thought I was overreacting. "It's just some glitch," he said, as he flipped the chicken on the stove. "23andme must've sequenced the DNA wrong, or mixed up the samples, or something."

"It's creepy though, isn't it?"

"Yeah, I guess." He opened the cabinet, rummaging around for plates. "But there's just so much room for error with that DNA stuff."

I tried not to think about it. But my night was plagued with nightmares of G—a faceless woman, calling from the forest. Who had my long dark hair and tall stature. A second mother who, somehow, had given me her DNA.

When I woke up, though, I realized something. If I shared 50% of my DNA with my father, and my mother, *and* G—well, 50% + 50% + 50% did not equal 100%.

One of my parents had to share DNA with G.

I called my mom on the way to work. "Did you see anyone listed in your DNA relatives named 'G'?" I asked, as I pulled onto the highway.

"G?" she repeated.

"Yeah. There's just... a person named G who keeps popping up on my DNA relatives."

"I don't think so," she replied. "But I don't know.

The website is kind of hard to use. Brandon was helping me with it."

"Could you ask—"

"Yeah, sure. Gotta go now, though."

With that being a dead end, I decided to bite the bullet and send G a message. Most likely, it'd be some big misunderstanding. G was probably some stranger living on the other end of the country with no connection to me whatsoever.

Hey, I noticed 23andme listed you as a relative. Do you have any family members with the last name T--- or K---, especially in the northwest US? Are you related to my mother, Agnes T---?

The response came less than an hour later. And when I read it, a slow chill ran down my spine.

you will find out soon enough.

That was the whole thing. The whole response. Those cryptic six words. I quickly shot a message back: **Are you related to me? Or my mom?**

No answer.

I stared at the screen, my heart pounding. Then, in one swift motion, I moved my cursor up and removed her as a connection. *Just a troll. A scammer. Something weird like that.*

A few days later, I checked 23andme again—to find that G had removed her account. Or, possibly, that the glitch had been fixed. Because G was no longer listed as my mother, or a relative at all.

Weeks went by and I forgot about the whole thing. Work got busy, gardening season was in full swing, and my hours were spent either working late in the office or slaving over my plant babies. I didn't even give G a second thought—

Until, one morning, it all came crashing down.

Two pink lines. My husband and I spent the morning crying, hugging each other, overjoyed about this little person we would bring into the world.

Until I went to the mailbox.

Inside was a folded piece of pink paper, tied off with black ribbon. No stamp—it must've been hand delivered. My throat went dry as I flipped it open and read the words on the page.

meet me at h--- park at midnight tonight.
-G

Of course I wasn't going to meet G in the park at midnight. That sounded like a good way to get murdered. "But I *am* really curious," I said to my husband Danny. "Do you think she's my mom's sister, or twin, or something?"

"I think the bigger question is how she knew where we live," he replied, shaking his head. "I still don't understand why you won't file a police report."

"I don't think you can file a police report for someone sticking something in your mailbox."

"But it's not *just* that. She messaged you creepy stuff on 23andme, right?"

"Just that one message."

"Yeah. See? That *with* the letter could be enough for a police report." Danny sat down at the table, facing me. "It's freaking weird, Kayla. We should call someone."

I bit my lip. He was right. But say G was some weird stalker, or something. She wouldn't be able to falsify her DNA records to match mine. It was more likely that she was a long-lost relative, who decided to find me after our brief messaging on 23andme. Unfortunately, my last name is pretty unique. And I'd given it to her right in the message I sent her. All she had to do was search for Kayla T---, filtering by northwestern states in the US, and she would find my address.

"People were saying online that if Mom had an identical twin, she'd show up as my mother, too."

"I thought you said her ancestry wasn't the same as your mom's, though."

"It's not. But apparently 2% Scandinavian ancestry is such a small amount, it could just be an error." I looked at my phone and sighed. My mom still hadn't called me back. I'd told her I wanted to talk about G... which, in retrospect, was probably a mistake.

Well, there was nothing to do now but wait for her call.

We went to bed at 10, but I couldn't sleep. My mom hadn't called me back all day, which was really uncharacteristic for her. The dread in the pit of my stomach grew. *Mom's lied to me my entire life. She has a sister. An identical twin.*

Why didn't she tell me?

And where has G been all these years? Did my grandparents give her up for adoption, when they were young? Did she run away and grow up in a foster home?

The entire thing was making my head spin.

I must've drifted off at some point, because the next thing I knew, I woke with a start. I stared into the darkness, unsure what had woken me. But then I heard it.

Thump, thump, thump.

Someone was knocking on the door.

My heart plummeted. I glanced over at Danny—but he was fast asleep. The clock read 1:11 AM. Swallowing, I pulled myself out of bed.

It has to be G.

I'm not going to open the door. I'm just going to look out the window.

The only window that overlooked the front porch was the one in the guest bedroom. Slowly, I tiptoed across the hallway, careful to not make any noise that could be heard from outside. I crouched in front of the window, and with a deep breath, swung the blinds away.

I couldn't see that much of her. The porch roof obscured her top half. But I could make out a plain black skirt, trailing to the floor. And, beneath that...

Bare feet.

Bare feet caked with dirt and mud. I glanced to the driveway, to the street—but didn't see any cars, other than our own and the neighbors'. *Did she walk here? In bare feet? From the park? Four miles away?*

Thump! Thump! Thump!

More knocking. Louder. Quicker. Insistent.

I crouched there, my legs aching, holding my breath. Something about this felt very, *very* wrong. Instinctively my shaking hands found my stomach. Thinking of my little baby.

THUMP! THUMP! THUMP!

I finally pushed myself into action. I ran across the hallway and woke Danny. While he was slowly getting up, I grabbed my phone and dialed the police. After they assured me someone was on the way, I walked back to the guest bedroom and pulled the blinds back.

She wasn't on the porch anymore.

For one wonderful, relief-inducing second, I thought she'd left. That she'd given up on me and decided to walk home.

But then I saw her.

She was standing in the darkness of our front yard.

And she was looking straight up into my window.

Maybe I should've run. Maybe I should've hidden in the bedroom with Danny until the police came. But something came over me. Maybe my first wave of maternal instinct. That I had to protect my baby at all costs.

I yanked the window open. "Hey!" I shouted. "Get the *fuck* off my property! I called the police!"

Now that my eyes had adjusted to the darkness, I could see her better. I could see her face. She looked *nothing* like my mother.

"HEY!" I screamed, my voice cracking. "Did you hear me?! The police will be here any second!"

She stared at me.

Then she slowly stepped towards the house. She didn't stop until she was right underneath my window.

She tilted her face up to look at me, her head at almost a ninety-degree angle with her body.

Then she smiled.

"The police may be able to chase me away," she whispered, so quietly I could barely hear it over the wind. "But they won't be able to save your baby."

Then she turned on her bare heel and walked away.

I watched her disappear into the darkness, my entire body shaking. Danny joined me a few seconds later, and he wrapped his arms around me, telling me everything would be okay. But I couldn't shake off the feeling that something horrible was going to happen.

They won't be able to save your baby.

The police took our statement. They weren't able to find the woman, but assured us they'd keep looking. Since she visited, I haven't been able to focus. Haven't been able to sleep. Because of my fears about my baby...

And because of something else.

As I watched her walk away that night, I noticed she had a birthmark just above her right elbow.

Just like I have.

I took the day off work. I'd barely slept—I kept thinking she was going to come back. When I finally got up for the day, though, I realized the situation was probably a lot less creepy than I thought. She wasn't some long-lost relative or Rumplestiltskin baby stealer. She was under the influence of drugs, or suffering from mental illness.

Those were the only explanations.

Of course, that didn't explain the DNA results. Or how she knew I was pregnant. But I forced all those nagging questions out of my head and tried to move forward. By the afternoon, I was feeling much better about the whole thing.

Then the bleeding began.

And my entire world came to a stop.

I began to sob. *No, no, no. I can't lose the baby. I can't.* My mom had told me once about the miscarriage she'd had, before my brothers and I were born. How it had nearly destroyed her. I thought I'd understood how horrible that was for her; but now, as I sat there staring at the smear of blood on toilet paper, I knew I hadn't *really* understood. Until now.

I called Danny. He left work immediately. We called the doctor, and they told me to go on bedrest. But deep down, I knew it wouldn't help.

They won't be able to save your baby.

She knew. She knew I was pregnant. She knew my baby was going to be lost forever.

She wasn't just some crazy woman. She *knew*.

The shrill ring of my phone snapped me out of my daze. I grabbed it—and my heart leapt as I saw the name on the screen. "Mom," I cried. "I've been trying to call you all day." Before she could say much else, I told her everything. The pregnancy. G visiting in the middle of the night, trying to break in. And the impending miscarriage...

"Kayla..." she started—and there was something

about her voice that made my heart drop. "You need to find her."

"What?"

"There's so much I haven't told you." Her voice shook as she spoke. "Her name... is Grezel. She came to me when I was eight weeks pregnant with you. The doctors were having trouble finding your heartbeat, and I thought I was going to have another miscarriage.

"She offered me a deal. She would be able to save you, but in return... you would carry some of her DNA. I don't know how she did it. I don't know why. I just knew that I was scared, and desperate, and willing to do anything to save you. Even if it sounded completely crazy.

"I met her in the woods. We did this sort of... I don't even know. A blood ritual? That's the best way I can describe it. I don't believe in witchcraft or anything like that, but whatever she did, it *worked*. A few days later, when I went to my appointment, you were fine."

I waited for her to say more, but she didn't. I was frozen, with the phone up to my ear, heart racing in my chest.

"Wait." The gears spinning in my head finally caught. "But she has to be related to you. The DNA test said I'm fifty percent you, and dad, *and* her. So there's got to be overlap."

"I don't know anything about that," she said. "I just know that she'll save the baby."

"But... I have no way of contacting her. What if she doesn't come back?"

A pause. Then: "She'll come back."

After the call, I just sat there. Staring at the wall. Trying to process everything she told me. Why did Grezel share DNA with my mom? Did she somehow... steal it... during the blood ritual? Maybe she was some sort of inhuman creature, that needed to suck DNA off everyone else. Maybe that was the trade.

This was starting to sound like some twisted fairy tale. One of the uncensored ones, where everyone dies horribly.

My mom was right. A few hours later, I was interrupted from my thoughts with a loud *thump! thump! thump!* on the front door.

I ran down the stairs as fast as I could. But when I swung the door open, Grezel wasn't standing there. Instead, there was another piece of pink paper. Scribbled in black marker were the words:

meet me in the woods behind the r--- mall at midnight. come alone.

-G

The forest was dark. I heard the chittering of bats overhead, somewhere, as they swept through the air for their nightly meal. The leaves crunched under my feet as I continued further in.

Just as I was starting to lose hope, I saw her.

A dark silhouette, standing in a small clearing off to my right. Wearing a long, black gown that draped so effortlessly over her body it looked like it was made of shadow. Her dark hair, streaked with silver, cascaded down her back.

"Grezel," I called out.

She turned around. Her skin was so pale in the moonlight, it looked like it almost glowed. "I see you've decided to join me."

"Can you save the baby?"

Her lips twisted into a crooked smile. "Yes," she crooned. "Come closer."

I slowly stepped towards her, my heart hammering in my chest. Up close, I realized she appeared older than I thought she was. Deep wrinkles cut her face, crinkling around her eyes. And her eyes... there was something off about them. Her irises were pure black—and they were too large, giving them an almost bug-like appearance.

"Are you ready to begin?"

I nodded.

She pulled a knife from the folds of her dress. The silver blade glinted in the moonlight. She smiled at me, crookedly, and drew it along her palm.

Then she grabbed my right hand. Turned it over. I let out a soft cry of pain as she dug the blade into my skin. Dark blood bloomed out of the wound, glinting in the moonlight.

Then she pressed her palm against mine.

A tingle of pain shot up my arm. I could feel it, feel *something*, traveling up my veins and deeper into my body. Then it dissipated, and we were standing there together, staring at each other in the darkness.

"Your child will live," she whispered.

"And they'll be okay? You're not going to take them from me, or—"

"Did I take you from your mother?"

I shook my head.

She turned around, her black dress swirling around her. "We are done here."

But something didn't sit right with me. It was... too easy. What did Grezel get out of all this? My DNA? Why would she want to save my baby? Just to genetically be their mother? Not to steal them or raise them as her own?

"Wait!" I called out. "There's got to be something you're getting out of this."

She turned back towards me, her wild dark hair falling in front of her face.

"What's the catch? Tell me. I don't want to spend my whole life dreading it."

She paused, her smile growing wider.

And then she spoke.

"Your children will carry my DNA. So will your brother's children. And so will your grandchildren, and your great-grandchildren, and your great-great-grandchildren. My DNA will lay dormant in them, spreading silently, generation by generation." Her smile grew wider. "Then, one day—when I am ready—my soldiers will come out of dormancy. And we will reclaim the forests and rivers, the earth that you destroyed. The earth that belongs to the fae."

Then she turned on her heel and walked deeper into the forest, until the shadows swallowed her up.

NEVER HAVE I EVER

I'm in college. Last night, I played the most disturbing game of Never Have I Ever with my roommates.

If you don't know the game, it goes like this: everyone holds up five fingers. You go around the room, saying "never have I ever" followed by something you've never done. Everyone who's done that thing has to put a finger down. Five fingers down and you lose.

Anyway, last night we'd been drinking a bit, and a lot of juicy secret-sharing was going on. We'd learned Tina and Layla had been skinny-dipping, I'd cheated on a test, and now... Layla had been in a threesome. "You had a threesome?!" Erin gasped. "Who? Who was it?"

"She doesn't have to tell. That's not part of the rules," Tina said.

"But... but..." Erin pouted. "Okay, fine. My turn. Never have I ever... had sex outside."

"You know, if you keep doing sex ones, I'm going to

lose in like two seconds," Layla said, adjusting her glasses.

"Okay. I'll do something different," Tina said. She leaned in closer and lowered her voice to an almost-whisper. "Never have I ever... seen someone die."

An uneasy silence settled over us. Our smiles faded and we glanced at each other. Then Erin and I each put our fingers down.

"Going with the creepy theme here," Layla said, "never have I ever used a Ouija board."

Erin and I put our fingers down again.

It'd been back in September. Shortly after that girl, Lucy, disappeared. One year above us, majoring in Art History. Looking back on it, it wasn't the most respectful thing to do. She was dead, probably. And here we were making some spooky thing out of it.

Although, not to shift blame, but it really was Erin's idea.

"Your turn," Layla said.

"Right. Okay." My throat was dry. I reached over and took a sip of my grasshopper. "Never have I ever smoked pot."

Then it was Erin's turn. She spun off mine, saying she'd never smoked a cigarette. And then we were back to Tina.

For a second, she didn't say anything. We all stared at her, and she stared back, her eyes nearly black in the dim light. She was smiling, slightly, as she looked at all of us. Hesitating, ramping up the tension.

"Never have I ever... killed someone."

Dead silence. Then Layla finally spoke, forcing a

laugh. "What the fuck?" she asked, crossing her tattooed arms over her chest. "Of course none of us have ever—"

She stopped mid-sentence.

And then she pointed at Erin.

"You... you had three fingers up before," she said, her voice weak. Small.

I looked at Erin. She sat there, stone-faced, holding up her pinky and ring fingers. She surveyed Layla with her cold blue eyes, then shook her head. "No I didn't."

"You totally did. Did you... kill someone?"

Erin narrowed her eyes. "If I did, do you really think I'd be stupid enough to put down a finger?"

Tina and I glanced at each other, eyes wide. "Uh, Layla," I finally cut in. "I'm sure she had three fingers up before."

"You sure? You saw her?"

"No, I didn't see her, but I mean... obviously, she didn't kill anyone."

Layla focused back on Erin. "You put one down for the Ouija board, and one for seeing someone die. What was the third one for?"

"Skinny dipping," she replied, without hesitating.

"No. Wait," Tina cut in. "That doesn't make sense. You said you don't know how to swim. That's why you wouldn't come with us to Lake Crystal."

"So? You can skinny dip without swimming. That's why it's called skinny *dipping*, not skinny *swimming*."

But I could hear it in her voice. She was getting flustered. My stomach twisted and my heart began to pound. *No. There's no way.*

Is there?

There was no way Erin killed someone. And even if she had, there was no way she'd admit it in a game of Never Have I Ever. The whole thing was ridiculous.

But then why is she acting so... weird? Why isn't she just laughing it off? My hands were shaking now. I looked at Layla, and Tina, and they both looked just as terrified as I was. *Maybe she did kill someone. Maybe...*

Something was bothering me. Nagging at the back of my mind. Something I thought was insignificant when it happened, but now, seemed very significant.

"I don't want to play anymore," Erin said abruptly. She got up off the floor and set her drink down on the table. "You guys are being too weird." She started down the hallway, where her and my bedrooms lay.

"Wait."

I stood up. She slowly turned around. "What, Caroline?" she asked, her eyes empty. "You going to accuse me of murder too?"

"No. Just... where were you that night? The night Lucy went missing?"

"Excuse me?" she spat.

The gears were turning in my head. Before, I hadn't put the pieces together. It wasn't weird for Erin to be out that night. I'd been out all night, at Jared's place or at a party, and so had Tina and Layla.

And yet...

It wasn't a weekend night. It was just a random Wednesday, around 2:00 am, when I heard Erin's door creak open next to mine. Heard her footsteps, thumping down the hall. I'd woken again with a start around 4:00 am, to hear her coming home.

Later that day we'd heard Lucy was missing.

"Where were you?" I asked, again. "I heard you leave. Around 2 AM. It was the night she went missing."

Erin's expression blanked.

Then, in an instant, she ran down the hallway. She pushed me aside, roughly, and I fell to the floor. My head made a sickening *thwack* as it hit the floor. Distantly, I heard the other girls scream. Above me, I saw the door swing open...

And then slam shut.

I scrambled up. But it was too late. By the time I peered into the hallway, she was already gone.

No one has found Erin yet. I don't know what happened to Lucy, and I don't even know if she's guilty. But I wonder if she didn't actually mean to put her finger down during our game. If maybe, she did it without thinking, on instinct.

Or, if maybe—

Something unseen forced her finger down.

FACEBOOK IS SHOWING ME MEMORIES I DON'T REMEMBER HAVING

If you're on Facebook, you'll notice they sometimes show you throwbacks they call "memories." Old photos you posted. Old status updates. That kind of thing.

Usually, they're super cringey. At least they are for me, anyway. I used to be one of those college girls that posted EVERYTHING on Facebook. Song lyrics that were a pointed *message* to an ex. Desperate updates fishing for compliments. And heaps and heaps of selfies, from every angle, every expression, every hairstyle.

I'd always look at them though. Some weird mix of nostalgia and morbid curiosity. Or at least, I used to—until they started getting creepy.

The first 'memory' that seemed off was a photo from May 3, 2013. I was sitting at the bar, wearing a navy blue tank top with little polka dots.

Except I didn't remember ever owning a shirt like that.

You might think that doesn't sound very creepy. But

I remember almost every clothing item I wore in college. I don't know if it's because I have a photographic memory, or because I was very into fashion. But I remember everything: the tight red sweater that was really flattering but a little itchy, the denim miniskirt that I couldn't fit into after I gained the Freshman 15, and the t-shirt that read 'Nothing But Net' with an old-timey '90s computer on it.

I had no memory of this shirt.

Maybe I borrowed it from a friend?

But that wasn't the only weird thing. There were no likes or comments—not a *single* one. And I didn't recognize where the picture was taken. Clearly it was some sort of bar—but it definitely wasn't *Victorious,* the bar we usually went to. I stared at it for a while longer, but eventually I had to click out of it and get on with my day. Soon after, I forgot about it.

Until the next day.

Another memory popped up. Without even thinking, I clicked on it. But as soon as I did, my heart began to pound.

This one wasn't a photo. It was a status update.

1:43 AM, May 4, 2012
i don't want to live like this anymore.

In of itself, that wasn't so weird. I often posted cryptic status updates. Sometimes trying to drop a covert insult on an ex, other times trying to sound "deep."

What was odd, though, was the date.

In May 2012, I was a sophomore. And I had recently entered the best relationship of my life. So it made absolutely *no* sense that I would be posting something like this.

Maybe I was referring to my classes or something? But I remember that semester, clearly. David and I had started going out. We were in the honeymoon phase, completely enamored with each other. And my classes that semester were pretty good too. I remember taking a class on folklore and urban legends in the English department.

So why did I post... this?

I shook my head. There was no way I could remember every single status update I'd posted ten years ago. Maybe I was just feeling down. Maybe I'd gained weight (I'd struggled on and off with an eating disorder), or maybe one of the cliquey girls in my dorm had been mean to me. College was an emotionally tumultuous time for me, honestly.

So, again, I just pushed it out of my mind and focused on other things. But then, just a few days later, there was another one.

You have a new memory to look back on today! the site told me cheerfully. But when I clicked on it, all the air sucked out of my lungs.

It was a photo of my hand.

With an engagement ring.

I'm not married. I've never been engaged. *What the hell?*

I stared at the post. It was dated May 7, 2014—only a few weeks before David and I broke up. I looked at the likes and the comments. Unlike the other two posts, this comment had one "like" on it.

From David.

But I blocked him. Right after the breakup. I went into my settings to double check, and there was his name on the block list. Usually when you block someone, you aren't able to click on their name—if they appear at all.

But when I went back to the memory, I was able to click on his name and see his profile.

And my stomach fell through the floor when I saw *myself* in his profile picture.

I was smiling, leaning into him, my arms wrapped around his. Wearing a new pair of glasses I'd never seen before. Wearing an outfit I'd never seen before.

But clearly wearing a wedding ring.

I scrolled through the profile, but everything else was hidden. No other photos, no relationship status, nothing. My mind scambled through the options—*is this some sick sort of joke? Maybe the profile is fake. Maybe the photo is photoshopped or AI-generated or something.*

I mean, there was no way it could *actually* be David. When he broke up with me, he didn't hate me, he wasn't vengeful. He was just... indifferent to me. Couldn't care less about me. Which hurt more than anything.

And also meant he wouldn't go through such lengths to prank me. I was the furthest thing from his mind, I'm sure.

I sucked in a breath and clicked *Send Message*.

The little message box popped up. My hands hovered over the keys. For a while, I couldn't decide what to say. Finally, I typed out something semi-coherent: *Hi. I don't know who this is, but your joke isn't funny.*

And it's kind of creepy honestly. Please take me out of your profile pic. Thanks.

The message went through... and then, a few seconds later, was marked as "Seen."

My heart pounded in my chest. But no reply came. He wasn't typing or anything. It was just... blank. I waited and waited, but nothing came. I stared at the screen so long, there was a nice little afterimage burned into my retinas.

Finally, I slammed the laptop shut and stormed off.

I thought that would be the end of it. That the message would scare them off and they would leave me alone.

But it was just to opposite. From the minute I sent that message... everything began to fall apart.

Later that evening, when I got out of the shower, there was a thin, red line on my left ring finger. Like I'd taken off a ring that was slightly too snug. When I woke up this morning, the left side of the bed felt warm.

Like someone had just been laying there.

I tried to ignore it. Both things were easily explainable... weren't they? I take really hot showers and my skin often gets blotchy red. I must've been lying on that side of the bed, before I woke up.

Nothing to worry about. Everything is fine.

But I can't ignore the text I got tonight. The text that arrived on my phone at 11:21 PM, from an unknown number.

Hey babe. Missing you <3 can't wait to be back home tomorrow.

IF YOU SEE A LIGHT ON THE WATER, RUN

It happened at Morgan's party.

Her parents had a mansion at the edge of the lake. We were down at the shore, dipping our toes in the water, drinking mojitos. Arun, Mabel, John, and me.

We'd just graduated from high school, and the entire world was at our fingertips.

Sometimes I wonder what would've happened if we didn't go. Would we be safe? Would our lives be normal? I guess it doesn't matter. We chose to go—and that was the night everything changed.

It was near 1 AM, I think. The flames danced, sending long shadows across the sand. The scent of burnt wood and booze wafted through the air. It was a moonless night, and the houses across the lake were dark.

People were hanging out in their own little groups, laughing and whispering and lighting joints. We were down by the shore, feeling the cool water roll over our feet, reminiscing about our final weeks of high school.

Then Mabel asked:

"What's that?"

We all looked up.

There was a light in the distance. Maybe a hundred yards away from us, straight across the lake. With how dark it was, it was impossible to tell if it was floating above the water—or if it was on the opposite shore.

"Maybe it's like, one of those will o' the wisp things?" I asked.

"I thought you only got those in swamps," Mabel replied.

"Oh shit you guys, it's a UFO! *Aliens!*" John imitated that guy in the History Channel meme. We rolled our eyes and laughed.

But still, I couldn't take my eyes off it. Neither could the other three. We watched it in uncomfortable silence, and then I realized—it was bobbing up and down, slowly. As if it were attached to a buoy in the water, or held by someone who was slowly walking towards the shore.

"Maybe someone's on the other side of the lake? With their phone flashlight on, or something?" Arun asked, squinting in the darkness. "Maybe we woke them up?"

"Yeah, but then, wouldn't the house be lit up?" I asked.

"Nah. If they got half a brain, they'll keep the lights off. That way, no one can see 'em." John shrugged. "It's what I'd do."

The way it bobbed up and down was... calming, almost. Hypnotic. It made me think there was no way it was a person. It was too perfect. *Must be some sort of lantern or something.*

But it hadn't been on before. Something must've triggered it. Maybe it was a lamppost on the shore with a motion trigger. But then, that didn't explain the bobbing...

"So weird," Mabel said, shaking her head.

"There's no way they can see us, right?" Arun asked, tapping nervously on the mojito glass in his hands. "I mean, we're too far away, right?"

"Yeah. No way they can see us," I replied.

And then the light went off.

Just like that, we stopped talking about it. Mabel started talking about how she and John would be leaving for U of Miami at the end of August. My heart hurt, knowing Arun was going to Stanford and I'd be thousands of miles away, attending the state college. I held Arun's hand a little tighter, trying to hold onto this memory forever. Just sitting next to him, feeling him breathe, under a sky filled with stars.

"Oh my gosh, it's freezing out here," Mabel said, hugging herself. "I'm gonna go to the car, get my jacket. You guys need anything?"

"Nah, we're good," John said, giving her a wave.

But just a minute or two after she left, the light blinked back on.

And it was halfway across the lake.

"Look—*look!*" I grabbed Arun's arm. "It's coming towards us!"

"Oh no. It's a boat. A police boat. They're coming to bust us." He dumped his mojito in the sand and got up.

"Relax. The police would just come to the house. They wouldn't come over on a boat," John replied, rolling her eyes. "What, you scared you're gonna lose your little spot at *Stanford?*"

"Oh, fuck off," Arun replied.

I glanced at the other partygoers. Most were oblivious, but a few were pointing to the shore. The light continued towards us, maybe 50 yards away now, blaring white. Unblinking.

A chill ran down my spine. "Who'd be on a boat so late?" I asked, getting up and brushing the sand off my legs. *Maybe it's a bunch of weird guys.* I mean, most of us in attendance were women, and we'd practically had a spotlight on us with the bonfire. Maybe they'd been idling out there in the dark water for hours.

Watching us.

But they'd be stupid to take us on, right? There were like 30 people here, some of them guys, athletes even.

Unless...

Unless they had a gun.

The light grew closer. "They're coming right at us," John said, the usual laughter in his voice gone. The chatter had died down, and a few others were picking up their stuff and heading for the stairs.

"Where's Mabel?" John asked, scanning the crowd.

I looked around, too. "I guess she's still at the car. We'll go up and tell her."

The three of us jogged through the sand to the wooden stairs that made the climb up to Morgan's mansion. Behind us, the chatter picked up again, but confused, distressed. I heard Morgan shout to someone: "Put out the fire! *Now!*" And then she was shouting "get inside!" over and over.

When we got halfway up the stairs, I looked back.

The light was still on. Hovering there, a few feet above the water, reflecting placidly in the dark water.

When everyone was inside, Morgan told us to keep the lights off and as she ran around locking the doors. I ran over to the living room and peered out the front window. But Mabel wasn't by the car anymore.

Oh shit.

I swung the front door open. "Mabel? Mabel? Get inside! There's someone out there!"

Nothing.

I ran back to John and Arun. "She's not out there." I scanned the crowd, huddled in the dark kitchen. But I didn't see Mabel's bleach-blonde hair or bouncy skirt anywhere among the silhouettes. My throat went dry.

"Oh, no no no, you think she's still out there?"

John was freaking out. So was Arun. The three of us ran over to the window. *Fuck.* The light was closer now. *Much* closer. Maybe only twenty feet from the shoreline. I scanned the beach, but it was too dark. The campfire was only smoldering embers. And strangely, the light from the boat—or whatever it was—didn't actually illuminate the shore in front of it.

I cracked the window open. "Mabel?!" I screamed. "Mabel, get inside, there's someone out there!"

And then I heard something.

A soft *thump-thump-thump* on the wooden stairs.

And when I squinted, I could see Mabel's bleached hair sticking out among the dark shadows. She was at the bottom of the stairs, quickly running up—

The light hit the shore. I could only tell it had, because it was so close to the remains of the fire. I scanned the stairs—Mabel was almost halfway up. "*RUN!*" I screamed out the window. "Mabel, *RUN!*"

For a moment, the light just hung there. Suspended in the darkness.

Then it moved.

It bobbed up and down, swinging slightly. Like a pendulum, like it was connected to something by a string. Heading straight for the stairs.

My eyes shot to Mabel—and my heart sunk to my stomach.

She'd stopped.

"Why'd she stop?!" John ran over and wrenched the window wide open. "Mabel! *RUN!*"

But she didn't.

I could see her clearly now, her silhouette halfway blocking the light below her. She was about halfway up—and she was just standing there, frozen, staring down at it. The light had stopped following her and just hovered there on the shore, a few feet above the sand. Completely still now. Not even bobbing.

And then she took a step down.

Towards it.

John leapt into action. He ran to the door—unlocked it—and swung it open. "Mabel!" he screamed.

When she didn't move, he started down the stairs.

I held my breath as I watched him approach Mabel. First he reached out and grabbed her hand. Tried to pull her away. When Mabel didn't budge, he grabbed her by the waist, picked her up bridal-style, and started back up the stairs.

The light shot into motion.

It jiggled and bounced as whatever was holding it raced up after him. Swinging wildly from side to side, growing larger by the second. I screamed with several others as it gained on him—it was going so fast, so *so* fast—

He burst in through the door. Slammed it shut, locked it, then set Mabel on the floor. "Close the blinds," he shouted. "*Now.*"

I glanced back. The light had stopped halfway up the stairs.

Just frozen there. Not even bobbing.

I reached up and grabbed the blind cord. The blinds fell with a metallic clang. Everyone else raced to do the same. My heart was pounding, and I kept staring at the lock on the door, making sure it was slid.

Then we were in darkness.

I ran over to Mabel. "Mabel? Are you okay?" I asked.

Her brown eyes stared up blankly at the ceiling.

"I think she's in shock or something," John said, lifting her slightly and cradling her head on his lap. "It was like... she was in a trance, or something. I couldn't get her to follow me."

Morgan ran over, breathing hard. "The police are on their way. I told them no one was hurt, but, but..." She trailed off as she looked into Mabel's blank eyes. "Oh, God, this is so horrible—"

"It's here! *It's here!*"

Someone was shouting. I whipped around.

No.

Light shone in through the blinds.

Slowly, it passed from left to right. Then it paused and turned around, slowly making its way to the other window. As if it were looking for a way in—

"Let it in."

We turned back to Mabel. Her eyes were no longer blank; they were wild. She shot up, scrambling to her feet. *"LET IT IN,"* she repeated, her voice a hoarse growl. *"LET IT IN LET IT IN LET IT IN!"*

She darted for the window.

John, Arun, and I all darted after her. I got there first, wrapping my arm around her waist, trying to tug her back.

But it was too late.

With a metallic *schliiing,* she pulled up the blinds.

The light shone in. Bright. Unwavering. Staring into my soul. I couldn't move, couldn't blink. All I could do was just stand there, frozen, with my arms around Mabel's waist.

Hypnotized.

And then I felt warmth in my heart. Exhilaration. Staring into the light filled my soul. It made me feel complete. Happy. At peace. It was the same warm feeling I got when I imagined Arun and I together forever. When I closed my eyes and just enjoyed being in his arms. It was beautiful, wonderful. Everything was right with the world.

But then—

Something caught my eye. A shape. Something floating in the darkness behind the light. It took me a second to recognize it, but then with heart-stopping horror, I did.

Teeth.

Rows and rows of pointed teeth, twisted into a grin. A Cheshire cat smile, floating in the darkness. The jaws of an anglerfish, floating in the deep ocean. What a fish sees seconds before its demise—

Schliiing.

Someone lowered the blinds. I blinked, rubbed my eyes, and looked confusingly around at the others. For many minutes, no one spoke.

When I finally looked back at the window, the light was gone.

Mabel was never the same after that. A few weeks into the summer, she went away to a mental institution. She didn't start at U of Miami in the fall. John went alone, and I recently saw photos of him with his new girlfriend on Facebook. Arun and I broke up as well, and I can't say I've enjoyed my first year of college without him.

But that's not the only wrong thing in my life.

You see, last night—just before I went to bed—I looked out the window.

And I saw a white light, deep in the forest, shining back.

SIDE EFFECTS

I picked up the prescription for Xamira on Monday.

The last IBS medicine made me vomit, so this time, I decided to check the side effect warnings on the bottle *before* I took it. With relief, I noticed it was small—just a few lines.

Xamira has no physical side effects. However, you may wish the side effects were physical.

I stopped. Reread the sentence.

You may wish the side effects were physical.

... What?

I turned the bottle over, looking for any other text. But no, that was it. I read the text a third time, and then a fourth. *What does that even mean?*

Should I call Dr. Lu? But he'd specifically recommended this medication, saying it helped his other patients with my symptoms—it's not like he chose it at random. I did a quick search online just in case, though.

But the only side effects listed online were things like *bloating* and *headaches*.

I wonder if the pharmacists can customize the text. I mean, they're the ones printing the labels, right? I snickered. *That's actually sort of funny. Not sure if it's legal or ethical to change the side effects of a medication, but... I gotta give him points for creativity.*

I downed one of the little white pills.

And it worked *amazingly*.

I had none of my usual symptoms. I didn't have a stomachache. I wasn't bloated. I wasn't in pain. I felt seriously amazing—better than I had in years.

I couldn't wait to get home from work and tell my husband all about it. How Dr. Lu had worked magic in finding me the right drug. How amazed I was at modern medicine. How the world looked suddenly beautiful again. Yeah, I know that sounds dramatic—and I know IBS isn't even *that* serious compared to other medical conditions. But still. When you live with discomfort and pain for a decade, and then one day, it's suddenly gone without a trace—it feels like a veil has been pulled up and the entire world looks brighter.

The house was empty when I got home from work. Doug told me he'd pick up our son Benjamin from his friend's on the way home, and they'd be back around 6. That gave me almost an hour. I decided to make dinner. Usually I followed a recommended diet for IBS, but not today. While the chicken was cooking on the stove, my phone began to ring.

"Doug!" I said. "You're not going to believe this! This new medication I'm on, it's—"

"Carrie?"

As soon as I heard his tone, my heart dropped. I knew something was wrong. Terribly wrong. I froze in the middle of the kitchen. The chicken sizzled on the stove. The pasta water bubbled softly.

"What—what's wrong?"

"It's Benjamin," he said, his voice starting to shake.

I couldn't move. Couldn't breathe.

"He... he..." Doug's voice broke. "The neighbors here, they have a pool, and—"

Oh no. Oh, God, please, no.

He kept talking but I didn't hear it. Ringing filled my ears. I lowered myself to the floor, no longer able to stand. *No... no. This can't be happening. This can't—*

"We're home!"

I whipped around.

The door was swinging open. And there was Benjamin, darting into the house, going straight for the TV. Doug following him, balancing a pizza box in his hand.

The phone clattered to the floor.

And when it did, the screen lit up.

It was just on the home screen. There was no ongoing call.

I ran over to Benjamin. Felt his face. He felt real. I scrambled back over to my phone and scrolled through the recent calls history. Nothing was there.

What... the... fuck?

"Carrie? Are you okay?" I heard Doug say. But his voice sounded so far away, over the rushing in my ears.

The medication. That little warning, on the side of

the bottle. *You may wish the side effects were physical.* Did the drug... cause hallucinations?

"I... I think I need to go to the hospital," I choked out.

As far as tests were concerned, I was fine. When I showed the doctor the pill bottle, and he came to the same conclusion I did. "Wow. The pharmacist must've changed the text." He shook his head. "He could lose his license for this."

"But the pills... they're definitely Xamira?"

"They certainly look like it. They have the little 'X 50' stamped on them. It would be hard for someone to fake that, unless they had access to a professional lab." He placed the bottle on the desk. "But, I'm still going to send it to the lab to get tested. It's possible they mixed a tiny bit of some hallucinogenic drug into the bottle, and shook it up so it'd stick to the pills." His eyes darted from mine, and he shook his head, looking thoroughly confused. "I just think we'd see some dust at the bottom of the bottle if he did that. And I didn't see any, at all."

They told me I could stay overnight, if I wanted to be monitored. But since I seemed completely lucid, they wouldn't force me. I decided to go home. I could tell the medication was already wearing off—the familiar stomachaches were rearing their ugly head. Hopefully, the hallucinations would go with them.

And the lab results of the pills would come back within 48 hours.

I spent the rest of the evening with Benjamin and Doug, so overwhelmingly thankful that I still had my wonderful little boy.

I woke up with a start.

My body was drenched in sweat. I strained my ears, listening, wondering what woke me up. I glanced over to Doug—but he wasn't there.

"Doug?" I called out into the darkness.

Nothing.

I glanced at the bathroom. No light under the door. Quietly, I pulled myself out of bed and tiptoed to Benjamin's room. He was sleeping peacefully in his bed, snuggled under his Paw Patrol blanket.

I was about to turn back to my room—when I heard a noise downstairs.

Something between a cough and a groan. I froze in the hallway, every muscle in my body suddenly on high alert. "Doug?" I whispered.

"Help," a weak voice called out from downstairs.

Doug's voice.

I ran down the stairs, my feet slapping against the wood. But I saw it before I even entered the kitchen—a pool of dark blood, seeping along the floor, oozing into the grooves of the tile. "Doug!" I screamed, breaking into a run—

He was slumped over in a chair. His shirt was covered in blood. "They... they broke in," he choked out, his voice growing weaker and weaker. "Call... police..."

No. This can't be happening.

I felt for my cell phone—but I'd left it upstairs. Panicking, I raced back up the stairs and darted into the room. I reached for my phone—

And stopped dead.

Doug was in bed. Snoring away.

It was just another hallucination. Doug... he's okay. I sucked in a shaking breath. The bottle of Xamira, I remembered, was a once-a-day pill. The effects probably didn't wear off until a full 24 hours had passed.

Shaking, I climbed back into bed with him. "I love you," I whispered, before rolling over and closing my eyes.

But I was wrong.

In the morning, I woke up to an empty bed.

I raced down the stairs. But I knew what I'd find, before I saw it: a pool of blood, now dark and dried. Shards of glass, scattered across the floor, glinting in the morning sun. A figure, slumped over in the kitchen chair.

"Mom?" I heard Benjamin call out behind me. But I couldn't move. Couldn't speak.

"Go... go back to your room," I choked out. "*Now!*"

The hallucination had been Doug. Sleeping peacefully in bed.

What I'd seen in the kitchen... had been absolutely real.

STREETLIGHTS BLINKING

I first noticed it in a Walmart parking lot.

The kids had too much energy, so we went for an evening Walmart trip. As we walked back to the car, I noticed one of the streetlights in the far corner, blinking on and off.

There's something about blinking streetlamps that's inherently creepy. I don't know why. Maybe because we're evolutionarily designed to be afraid of the dark? And blinking streetlights often go out? Or, maybe it's because of the stop-motion effect. There's a reason why haunted houses use strobe lights all the time.

In any case, I found myself staring at it as we helped the kids in the car.

And that's when I noticed something was... off.

As a car drove by on the main road, the streetlight blinked off--and there was something there, that obscured the red tail lights for just a split second.

It happened so fast, I thought I imagined it. Especially when the light blinked back on an instant later, and there was clearly nothing standing under it.

I didn't think much of it and got into the car. As we pulled out onto the main road, glanced back at it. It was still flickering, and something about it sent a chill up my spine.

We pulled out onto the road and the light disappeared from view.

The kids went right to bed, and then my husband and I were unwinding in the living room. I was flipping through pages on my Kindle when something caught my eye.

The lamppost outside our house was blinking on and off.

I walked over to the window. "What's up?" Charles asked behind me, when I'd been standing there a few minutes.

"The light's flickering."

"So?"

"There was a streetlight flickering in the Walmart parking lot, too." I turned to him. "Isn't that weird?"

"Not really."

He went back to his snacks. Pushing out the uneasy feeling in my stomach, I started to turn away--

Wait.

I turned back.

There was a light on in the house across the street.

But when the lamppost blinked off, the black edge of the window wasn't quite straight.

I squinted at it. There was a bump, or a curve-- almost like a semi-circle--that was poking into the golden square of the illuminated window. Like something was standing there, partially blocking out the window's light.

Except, nothing was there. Because the shape disappeared every time the light blinked back on.

"Charles. Come back over here."

"Do I have to?"

"I see something... weird, I don't know." I glanced back at him and frowned. He was leaning back in the recliner, feet up, stuffing himself with chips. "Please come over?"

"All right, all right."

He heaved himself off the couch and came over. I described the curve to him, the little sliver of silhouette I was seeing.

"I don't see it."

"You don't see it?"

He shook his head. "There's nothing out there, Becca."

I squinted again into the darkness. Then I gave up and settled back in with my book.

Something woke me in the middle of the night.

I rolled over and tried to go back to sleep. But then I heard it again. A distinct *thump* coming from somewhere in the house.

"Charles, I heard something," I said, shaking his shoulder. But I didn't wait for him to wake up. I flicked on the hall light and ran to the kids' rooms. My son, thankfully, was sleeping soundly. I leapt for my daughter's room—

And stopped dead.

In the crack under the door, I could see a flickering, bluish light.

I grabbed the doorknob and burst inside—

The nightlight. It was blinking on and off, erratically. Casting the entire room in jerky, stop-motion flashes. I ran over to the bed—thank God, my daughter was there, sleeping peacefully. I glanced back towards the hall, to look for Charles.

I froze.

There was a dark shape in the corner of the room.

I could only see it for a moment. When the night-light flickered out. As soon as it came back on, the corner was empty. My heart pounded in my chest—I stared at the corner—

Off.

The shape was there.

On.

It wasn't.

Off.

The shape looked like someone crouched in the corner.

On.

It looked... closer?

Off.

Oh God. It *was* closer.

On ...

The intervals were getting longer. I was paralyzed. My breath was stuck in my lungs.

Off.

Fuck. It was *halfway across the room.*

On ... ...

The light blinked on. Remained on. That didn't give me comfort—I couldn't see it. It could be anywhere. It could be right in front of my—

Off.

I screamed.

It was *right in front of me.* Filling up my entire vision. I backed away, putting myself squarely between my daughter and me—

Click.

Yellow light filled the room. "Becca?"

Charles stood in the doorway, bleary-eyed. I glanced around wildly—but the room was empty. The nightlight was still off.

I leapt forward and pulled it out of its socket. It clattered to the floor. Then I began to sob, as I told Charles everything.

The next day, the whole thing seemed ridiculous. What, I really saw some figure huddled in our house? That disappeared in the light? It made no sense. It was much more likely that I'd seen some sort of sleep paralysis demon, or my half-asleep brain misinterpreted shadows, or something.

But when I went into my daughter's room later, something caught my eye.

Three coarse, long black hairs, laying on the carpet.

And now, as the sun is setting, and the deep shadows of dusk are filling the house... I'm terrified to turn on any lights.

THE PORCELAIN LADY

Youth is wasted on the young.

I always thought that was a stupid saying... until I got old. Looking back on my younger years, I wasted so much time. Gave two years of my beauty and youth to a guy who was emotionally abusive. Spent nights alone in my room, listening to music, when I could've been out there meeting someone. You don't know what you've got until it's gone, I guess.

And it was gone. Well, almost. 37 years old. Time slipping through my fingers. A flower starting to wilt.

But then I met Whitney.

Whitney was 8 months older than me. And yet, she looked like she was 29. Acted like it, too—she was the "fun" one, bringing youthful enthusiasm to our mom group while the rest of us gulped coffee down by the gallon and looked like zombies. I couldn't figure out how she did it all. How she stayed so thin, how her face looked so beautiful, how she had the energy of someone just out of college.

One day, I brought my son over for a playdate, and while they were playing video games upstairs I asked her.

"How do you do it?" I asked, sipping on a tea. "You have like twice the energy I do. And you look *amazing*."

She let out a little giggle. "All about moisturizing," she said, "and drinking lots of water."

"*Moisturize meeee,*" I replied, imitating that centuries-old character from Doctor Who. She laughed. "But seriously. That's all it is? If I drink a gallon of water a day and buy some face cream, I'll look like you?"

Okay. I admit, I was subtly trying to get her to admit she'd gotten work done. Or that she had a full-time nanny while she slept ten hours a day. Because it wasn't fair. Standing next to each other, I looked like I had ten years on her. And if it was really Botox that worked its wonders, hell, maybe I'd give it a try.

"Okay, I'll let you in on a little secret."

I knew it. I leaned forward eagerly, waiting for her to spill.

Except there's no way I could've predicted the words that came out of her mouth.

"It's because of The Porcelain Lady."

I frowned. When she didn't elaborate, I asked, "What, that's like some beauty salon or something?"

She smiled and shook her head. "No."

I sat there, confused. But then it dawned on me. "The Porcelain Lady" sounded like it could be a euphemism for a drug. Like "Molly" and "Mary Jane" are. Now that I thought about it, wasn't using women's names for drugs kind of sexist?

"Oh. It's a drug," I whispered.

"I guess you could call it that," she said, still smiling.

What's that supposed to mean? Either it's a drug, or it isn't. But I took her response as being coy. As a little wink and nod, a subtle signal that I was supposed to pick up on, that *yes, it's a drug, but I'm too much of a lady to admit I'm actually doing drugs.*

"If you're interested, I can hook you up!"

Dread settled in my stomach. I'd never, *ever* done drugs. Not even weed. They kind of... scared me, to be honest. Like, what if I murdered someone because the drugs made me thing it was a rabid dog attacking me? What if it's like *Oculus,* where you don't know what's real and fake and you kill a whole bunch of people based on your own perception of things?

"Sorry, I don't really... do... drugs," I said, lamely.

"Oh, no, it's not a *drug* drug," she said. "I just meant that... well, nevermind. You're not interested." She waved her hand away.

"No! I *am* interested."

"Okay. How about this. Why don't you come over tonight, after dinner? I can tell you all about everything, and you can decide whether or not it's right for you."

"Um... okay? I guess I can do that."

But just when I was getting excited, she said something that sucked all the air out of my lungs.

"You know, you can even make money with this. I know a couple who retired at 30!"

Oh no.

It's an MLM.

Multi-level marketing. Pyramid scheme. I swallowed—if I showed up tonight, it would probably be a three-hour presentation on how to sell some beauty cream on Facebook. And how I had to pay two hundred bucks for the starter kit.

But.

Whitney looked *so* beautiful across the table from me. Blue eyes sparkling, not a single wrinkle on her face. Body rail thin, like she could land a modeling job this instant. Maybe this product... cream, diet pill, whatever... actually *worked*.

"I'll see you after dinner. Around 8?"

"That's perfect," she replied, shooting me a showstopping smile.

I did some Googling at home. But nothing came up for "The Porcelain Lady." Which was weird, because most beauty MLMs are all over Facebook, Instagram, TikTok. I mean, if there isn't a Facebook group you can invite random high school acquaintances to, is it even an MLM?

I drove over at ten 'til. When I pulled into the driveway, though, Whitney's house was mostly dark. *Maybe she forgot we were going to meet up,* I thought. But as soon as I got up to the door, it swung open and she gave me a big hug.

But when I stepped in... things seemed a little off.

The first thing I noticed was the smell. Like spices or

potpourri or something, but not in a good way. It was like sweet cinnamon and fresh pine and punchy cayenne all mixed together in a cake no one would eat.

Oh no. This better not be some essential oils crap.

Frowning, I followed her into the dining room. But, surprisingly, I didn't see any sort of display set up on the table. There was just a single tealight candle, flickering brightly in the dark house.

"Why don't you sit?" Whitney asked, taking a seat at the table.

"Oh, um, okay."

I sat across from her—and a chill went down my spine.

Whitney's face, lit in the harsh shadows of the candlelight, didn't look so pretty anymore. Deep shadows seeped into her eye sockets and the hollows of her cheeks, flickering and dancing as if her face were morphing before my eyes.

"Now, I want you to close your eyes..." she said, closing her own and taking a deep breath, "and imagine the end of your life."

"... What?"

"Imagine. You're almost 80 years old. It's hard to get out of bed. Your joints ache, all your friends are gone, and your skin looks like a shriveled prune."

I stared at her.

"You're not closing your eyes!" she said in a sing-song voice, as she took a peek at me.

"Um. Okay." I closed my eyes, even though it made me uncomfortable.

"How valuable are those last ten years? When everything you ever had is gone? Health, love, beauty. All gone." She took in another deep breath. "Are they even worth living?"

I was well acquainted with the fear-mongering, predatory tactics of MLMs. Body-shaming plus size women, telling them they'll never attract another man, unless they buy some pill or cream. Telling moms their children are surrounded by toxins, but essential oils will magically block them. *Buy this or your life will suck/your kids will die/everything will go kaboom* is a tried-and-true method for MLMs.

"I guess those years are still worth living," I said, still keeping my eyes shut. "I mean, I want to meet my grandkids, if I have any. And just... more time would be nice, even if I'm old. Even just watching TV or someth—"

"Okay, but what if you could trade them for something in return?" Whitney said, interrupting me. "Would you, for example, trade those last ten years, to be youthful for ten more years?"

What is she getting at? Does the pill or cream or whatever cause cancer or something? I was about to ask for clarification—when I heard a *thump* from behind me.

My eyes shot open.

My gaze immediately snapped onto the mirror, mounted on the opposite wall. And with horror, I realized there was someone there. Standing behind me.

At first, I only saw the face. Bone-white, starkly contrasting with the darkness. Then I saw the rest of them, and with horror, I realized they were wearing a mask. The white color of their face didn't match their skin.

Oh God. They're going to rob me, or murder me, or something.

I shot up and ran to the door. Surprisingly, Whitney didn't shout at me, or try to grab me and pull me back. I wrapped my fingers around the doorknob and pulled—

No.

The door was locked.

I scanned the locks. But there was some sort of lock with a keyhole, that she must've locked when I wasn't looking. I turned around, heart pounding. "Let me out."

"You have to meet the Porcelain Lady," Whitney replied, gesturing towards the figure that was steady approaching through the darkness behind us. She appeared to be a woman, wearing a tattered dress—but very tall. It was unlikely I could take both of them on.

Whitney grinned at me. "She can give you youth. Isn't that what you want?"

She's batshit insane. "If you don't let me out, I'm calling the cops," I breathed.

"How?" She reached into her pocket... and with a grin, pulled out *my* phone.

My throat went dry. I turned to the window. The houses across the street had lights on. I pounded my fist against the glass. "Fire! *Fire!*" I screamed, knowing that was more effective than shouting help.

But there were two layers of glass and an entire street between me and them. No one seemed to notice. Nothing happened. I whipped around.

The figure, the 'porcelain lady' I guess, was standing right behind Whitney now.

And that's when I realized there was something terribly off about her.

Her skin. Even in the low light I could tell it had a grayish, bluish hue to it. Like she'd been dead for weeks. And there were these things—these dark lines, almost like cracks, spiderwebbing across her arms, up her collarbone, up to her jawline where they disappeared under the mask.

Like her skin itself began to shatter.

But her mask was pristine. The features were dainty and smooth, expressionless and perfect, like a mannequin's. And its pure white color, the way it glinted in the candlelight...

It looked like porcelain.

She'd stopped now. Right behind Whitney. She stared out at me through those almond-shaped eyeholes, bottomless voids of pitch black.

"Are you ready to make the deal?" Whitney asked me, with manic glee.

I stared at both of them. I was trapped. The Porcelain Lady tilted her head as she examined me, but did not step forward.

"Okay... I'll make the deal," I said slowly, eyes flitting back and forth between them. "Ten years of my life for youth, right? I'll look twenty again?"

Whitney nodded.

"Okay. Okay, I'm in," I said, nodding, smiling. Trying to sell the lie. I stood there—and then I dashed to the left, towards the living room.

I sprinted through the darkness, towards the back door. I didn't even know if they were coming after me or not—my blood was pulsing in my ears, and all I could focus on was the singular goal of, *I have to get out of here, or I'm going to die.* I darted into the kitchen—and when I saw that same lock on the door, I ran to the nearest window and yanked it open.

Surprisingly, there was no extra lock. I reeled my knee back and prepared to kick out the screen—

A cold hand grabbed mine. My entire body spun backwards, away from the window. My head bobbed on my neck and I saw the room, spinning around me—

The Porcelain Lady.

Her face, in my vision.

Except her white mask of porcelain had been distorted. Stretched. Her mouth was a gaping wide hole, a black abyss, large enough to fit my entire head. I screamed and thrashed—but I felt a dizzying weakness spread throughout my whole body, like pins and needles, lighting up every neuron, every cell. But I forced myself to lunge—with all my energy, everything that I had.

And, miraculously, I broke away.

I dove for the window and I fell out, the screen popping out and falling underneath me. Then I scrambled up and, without turning back, raced across the grass to my car.

When I got home, I burst inside and locked all the doors. "What's wrong?" my husband asked, as he came down the stairs. "I just put Jackson to sle—"

He stopped dead on the stairs.

His mouth hung open, as he stared at me. "What?" I asked, as I turned away from the door—but somewhere, deep down, I already knew what he was going to say.

"You look... different," he said, still frozen on the stairs. "So... young."

WARNING: CONTENTS MAY CAUSE HAPPINESS

At first, the big red WARNING text on the envelope made my heart stop. But then, when I read the actual warning, I let out a groan.

WARNING: Contents may cause happiness.

That's about the stupidest marketing schtick I've ever seen. Rolling my eyes, I brought it inside.

It was small. *The perfect size and shape for some jewelry,* I thought, as I ripped the package open. It was my birthday tomorrow, and my sister Melissa always sent me a gift. Never anything elaborate or expensive, but always *nice.* Like artisanal soap, or a pair of earrings, or a cute nail polish.

I pulled out the little silver box. Lifted the lid.

A gold-toned locket sat in black velvet.

"Ooooh. Pretty," I said to myself, carefully lifting it out of the box. I clasped the chain around my neck, then looked in the mirror. It was perfect—not too big, not too small, and the perfect shade of gold for my olive skin tone.

Imagine my surprise when, later that day, I got another package. With a cute T-shirt and a gift message from Melissa.

If Melissa didn't get this... who did?

My mind immediately went to Greg. But of course he wouldn't send this—he'd already found someone new. He lived in my mind every day, creeping in at the most unexpected moments, in the dead of night, in the laughter of a familiar joke... and yet he probably never thought about me.

Is it possible he ordered this before we broke up?

It had only been six weeks. I couldn't imagine my mom, or Beth or Frankie, sending this to me.

My fingers caressed the locket. The smooth, cold, metal heart. The rather sharp clasp, holding the two halves together.

I'll ask around.

I'm sure it wasn't Greg.

After a week of questioning, I was no closer to finding out the sender.

That probably should've been reason not to wear it. For all I knew, some guy was stalking me, and he'd sent this to me to harm me. Dipped it in poison or rabies or something and was watching me right now from the bushes, waiting for me to die.

I figured, though, it was probably just a mix up. I

ordered things online often, and it was possible this was sent to me instead of the waffle maker I was still waiting on from eBay. Or maybe it had been addressed to the neighbors—I couldn't remember for sure whether it had actually said my name on the address label.

After a lot of thought, I sent a simple text to Greg. I probably shouldn't have, but I was curious. *Hey, I got this locket in the mail. Did you send it by any chance?* Predictably, he didn't reply.

Despite the mystery, I decided to keep wearing it. In fact, I even put a photo in it. I popped open the clasp—which was really too sharp for its own good—and the heart sprung open. I slipped a photo inside. A photo of myself. I told myself it was empowering, a declaration of self-love, the start of my journey to accepting myself.

Really, I was just lonely.

The picture was a black-and-white photograph I'd had taken when I was 21. Sort of a glamour shot. I wasn't smiling, and I wasn't looking into the camera. But my eyes looked big and dark and my soft curls fell perfectly around my face.

It was Greg's favorite picture of me.

I wore the locket most days. I don't know why—I just felt drawn to it. I hadn't treated myself to new jewelry in a while. It was a nice change from the hexagonal druzy necklace I usually wore. *Is that how Greg feels about me now? She's the shiny new thing, and I'm yesterday's news?*

I think her name was Katie or Carrie or Callie. One of those 'C' or 'K' names ending in -ie. She was cute—I'd seen her all over his social media. Long dark hair and tan skin. A killer smile. I hoped I'd never have to meet her.

Sadly, I was wrong.

It was three weeks after my birthday when I ran into them in Walmart. I was pushing a cart full of cereal and beans with my hair uncombed. He was giggling with her as they walked through the store. His eyes caught on mine—"...Sam?"

I stopped dead.

No no no this can't be happening—

"Uh, hi," I said, awkwardly.

"Hi," the girl interjected, smiling at me. "I'm Carrie."

My heart was pumping. I felt shaky. I could feel Greg's eyes staring at me. I looked awful. "Uh, sorry, I'm in a huge rush," I said quickly. "I have to make it back, because, yeah, uh..." I trailed off, gesticulating. "Nice seeing you!"

I pushed the cart forward.

And that's when it happened.

As I rushed past them as fast as I possibly could, the wheel of the cart caught on a display of sunscreen. The handle jabbed into my abdomen, kicking me off course, my body still moving with the momentum of my hurried walk-run of shame. I began toppling down and I thought *oh no, this is the most embarrassing thing ever—*

But instead of hitting the ground, I collided with Carrie.

She let out a yelp. The two of us hit the ground hard, me halfway on top of her. I immediately scrambled upwards, my elbow and side stinging with pain. "Oh no—I'm so, so sorry—"

I froze.

She was bleeding. Blood was dripping out from somewhere, a wound on her neck, spilling out onto the floor. I stood there, frozen, in shock. *What...?* Greg started shouting, rushing to her. A woman screamed. Somewhere, I heard someone on the phone with 911. But all I could do was stare, backing away, my brain unable to piece together what was happening.

When the police arrived and examined everything, they figured out pretty quickly what had happened. My locket had blood on it. In the fall, the sharp clasp holding the two halves together had pressed into her neck and punctured a vein.

Thankfully, she lived. But she stayed in the hospital for a night, and apparently lost a lot more blood than she should have. I was pretty shaken. After the whole thing, I just sat in the parking lot of the Walmart and cried for a long time.

When I got home, I ripped the locket off my neck, ready to throw it in the trash. But before I did, I opened it up to get the picture of myself out.

And when I did...

I *swear*, I looked like I was smiling.

STRIP MALL

My husband and I have a strange tradition. A few times a week, we go walk around our local strip mall at night. It's a way for our kids to burn off some extra energy before bedtime. Just a quick little trip, then right to bed.

Usually, a few stores are still open. But tonight, since it was Sunday, everything was closed. Still, we got the kids out and headed for the brightly-lit walkway.

"Ha, look," I said, pointing to the OPEN sign at the thrift store.

My husband shrugged. "Maybe they're still open?"

I peered in at the dark store, the still rows of clothing hanging in the darkness. "I doubt it."

We continued down the sidewalk, past the seamstress/dry cleaning place. Clothing hung behind the counter, and a huge sewing machine sat in the window, the needle piercing a beige square of cloth.

Ahead of us, one of the fluorescent lights was out. A patch of shadow, next to the butcher shop. We all stared in at the meats under the glass display, neatly packaged for tomorrow's customers. "Makin' me hungry," my husband said, and I laughed.

The next store was one that had been out of business for a long time. There was no sign—just a blank space of faded concrete, with the ghost of the words *BARBER*. The windows were papered over, but they weren't always. Several months ago I remember looking in, at the darkened hallway that stretched to the back, at the small piles of leaves and debris that pooled in the corners.

I wondered if the paper meant something was finally moving in.

"Come on, you can run faster than that!"

I looked up. My husband and our two boys had already run far ahead of me. They were almost at the end of the strip mall, at the Aldi. I took a final glance at the empty store, then ran after them.

The Aldi, which was usually open at this hour, was closed. Seeing the grocery store empty and dark was a little unnerving; usually it was bustling with shoppers, even late at night. We then turned around and continued back towards the other side of the mall, towards our car.

But when we passed the empty store again, I stopped.

There was a rip in the paper.

I stared at the window, my reflection looking back at me. Then I leaned forward. The rip was small, only about an inch wide. But it was big enough to see inside.

I leaned in. But I didn't see a dark, empty store on the other side.

I saw an eye.

I leapt back and screamed. My husband and the kids came running. I stared at the hole—but there was no one there. Just darkness. "I—I *saw* someone," I panted, pointing. "Someone's in there! Watching us!"

I grabbed the kids' hands and broke into a run, nearly dragging them. My husband, confused, paused for a second—and then broke into a run after us.

But as we passed the other stores, I saw... things.

The butcher shop. Someone was in there, standing at the meat table. His back was turned to us, but I heard the *thump! thump! thump!* as he brought the cleaver down on the slab of meat in front of him.

Then the sewing shop. There was someone sitting at the sewing machine; I heard the *ch-ch-ch* of the needle, threading up and down through the fabric. Except... was it fabric? Because as we passed, I realized the beige cloth was such an odd color. Pinkish beige... like the color of my skin.

And then the thrift store. I caught movement out of the corner of my eye—shapes, shadows, people moving towards the front door. Towards *us*. I pushed myself to run faster, my feet slapping against the sidewalk. The car was only twenty feet away... fifteen... ten...

I pulled the doors open and forced the kids inside. Then I dove into the driver's seat. But as I started the car, my heart plummeted like an anchor.

The strip mall was empty.

I didn't see my husband anywhere.

"David?" I screamed into the darkness.

But there was only silence.

I reported everything to the police. They didn't believe my story, but the more days that went by without him showing up, the more they had to admit he was actually missing. Theories like *mugging gone wrong, hit and run,* and *left for the mistress* were thrown around online and in town.

But I know the truth.

So please. I beg you. Never go to a strip mall after all the stores are closed.

Because, as it turns out, the stores aren't closed at all.

CHEESE

I found it on Monday.

I was cleaning out the fridge, and on the top shelf, I found a package of provolone cheese. It had seen better days: the package was open and there was greenish mold growing over the slices.

"Eugh." I immediately threw it out.

But two days later, I found a *second* package of moldy provolone. "Alex!" I shouted. "How many packages of provolone did you buy?!"

He sauntered in. "Uhh, I didn't buy any provolone."

"Not recently. I mean a long time ago. I found it all moldy in the back of the fridge." I frowned at him. "You shouldn't buy it if you're just going to let it rot."

"I *didn't* buy it. I never buy provolone," he replied, annoyed. "I hate how it tastes."

"Well, it's definitely not mine."

I let it go--but then I found the *third* package of provolone.

I stormed straight over to Alex. "Is this some kind of joke?"

"Huh?"

I dropped the cheese on his lap. "Eugh! Why would you—"

"This isn't funny! Stop messing with me!"

He gingerly picked up the cheese and went to the trash can. "Look, Rachel. That isn't my cheese, okay?"

"It isn't mine either!"

"Are you sure this isn't left over from the barbeque?"

"Yeah. I only bought American cheese for that."

"I don't know what to tell you. But I promise you, Rachel, I did not buy that cheese." He huffed and walked into the other room, going back to the TV.

Questions raced through my head. I didn't buy the cheese. Alex didn't either. And all the other options seemed far-fetched: one of us had a split personality who loved provolone cheese. Someone was living in our attic and using our fridge to store his cheese.

This whole thing was starting to get a weird.

For a week, there were no cheese-related incidents.

But then, on Tuesday, I was in a rush to get to work. And, lo and behold, as I raked through the middle shelf looking for my coffee creamer—I found another one.

Moldy provolone cheese.

I couldn't believe it. But I was late, so I chucked it into the trash and continued to work. And by the time I got home, I had a plan.

I spent two hours removing everything from the fridge. I searched through the items, and while I found some genuinely scary things—a piece of 10-day-old lasagna, moldy strawberries, and grape jelly that had been open three months ago—I found no provolone cheese.

"What are you doing?" Alex asked, when he got home midway through my cleaning.

"Cleaning the fridge." I didn't mention the cheese, because I thought it would lead to a fight. Besides, now it was over. I'd gone through everything and I knew, with 100% certainty, *there was no more cheese.*

That night, I slept soundly. I woke up early and headed down the stairs, smiling brightly. After drinking some water I stepped over to the fridge to find something for breakfast.

I swung open the fridge door—and screamed.

Every single item in the fridge was a package of moldy provolone cheese.

They were stacked on the shelves. Packed into the meat drawers. Flopping out of the door. Alex came running behind me, but as soon as he saw the fridge, he started screaming too.

"What... the... fuck?" he asked breathlessly.

"Someone's in our house. And they're fucking with us," I said frantically, backing away from the fridge. My heart was pounding in my chest, rushing in my ears so loudly I could barely hear my own voice. "That's the only explanation."

Alex reached over me and slammed the fridge door

shut. "Listen, Rachel," he said, his voice wavering. "I have to tell you something."

My heart dropped.

He glanced around, avoiding my eyes. "I bought the provolone cheese."

"What?!"

"Remember when we were babysitting Emma two months ago? Lily said she liked sandwiches, so I bought meat, and bread, and the provolone cheese. I totally forgot about it until a few days ago, when she called me. But I *swear*," he said, finally looking me in the eyes, "I have no idea where the other ones came from. I only bought the one package."

"Why didn't you tell me?"

"Because I didn't want you to think that I was trying to play some sort of mind game with you. I *swear*, Rachel, I didn't do this." He reached for his pocket and pulled out his phone. "I'm calling the police."

"You're saying that... you woke up to find the contents of your fridge... replaced with cheese." The officer finished scratching his notes, then looked between us. "Is that correct?"

"I know it sounds crazy," I said.

"But someone must've broken in and put all this cheese in there. There's not... not any other explanation."

He sighed. "Do you have any friends that like to play pranks? Has anything like this happened before?"

We shook our heads.

"And no valuables were taken. Just the cheese."

We nodded.

The other officer joined us. "I didn't find any evidence of forced entry," she said. "Nothing seems out of place."

"Look, guys. I can understand how this might be scary. But I'm sure it's just some teenagers that snuck in somehow—through an open window, maybe—and thought this would be the most hilarious thing ever. And we'll find them," he added quickly, seeing our expressions of disappointment. "But I don't think you have anything to worry about here."

The officers left soon after that. Alex and I looked at each other. "Well, that was useless," he said to me, after shutting the door.

I had trouble sleeping that night.

Logically, I knew the officer's theory made the most sense. Whoever had put the cheese there probably didn't mean us any harm. After all, they could've murdered us in our sleep last night. At best, they were a stupid teenager looking for laughs; at worst, they were a weirdo that enjoyed playing mind games.

Mind games that, technically, didn't hurt anyone.

I double and triple checked the locks that night. But I couldn't fall asleep. Alex was able to drift off immediately; but I couldn't stop thinking about the cheese. And the longer I thought about it, the more holes I poked in the officer's theory.

Where would someone get that much moldy cheese? It must've been like 40 packages. Even if they bought out the entire Wess Market, it wouldn't be 40 packages.

And they wouldn't be moldy.

And now that I thought about it, all the packages I'd seen had roughly the same amount of mold. And the moldy splotches were in the same position.

It was almost like each cheese package was an exact replica of the others.

You're thinking about this too much. Just go to sleep.

But the thoughts didn't stop. *Where did all our other food go? Did someone just walk out with ten pounds of groceries? It would be really awkward and risky to break into someone's house and make multiple trips stealing that much food.*

And why had I never found my coffee creamer, after that day I'd found the fourth provolone? Had they stolen that, too?

All these questions spun round and round in my head until, finally, I fell asleep. But my sleep didn't last long.

I woke up with a start.

Even though I was half-asleep, I knew something was wrong. I forced myself up and looked around the dark room, straining my ears for sounds of an intruder. But everything was still and silent. I rolled over to go back to sleep—

No.

Oh, God, no.

Where Alex should've been sleeping, there was only a pile of moldy provolone cheese.

ADVICE FOR MY WEDDING NIGHT

My fiancé and I are getting married in two weeks. However, my mom just gave me some really weird advice for my wedding night, and now I don't know what to do.

My family isn't religious. But they're a very proper bunch. They believe in "good old-fashioned values," like: work hard and you'll achieve the American Dream (yeah right, in this economy), recognize your husband as head of the household (the 1950s called and want their misogyny back), and... of course... no sex before marriage.

So, my mom sat me down and decided to give me "the talk." Two weeks before my wedding. At 23 years old.

"I want to talk about your upcoming wedding... and the wedding night," she started.

My jaw nearly hit the floor. "Uh... okay?"

Talking about sex with my mom would be hard

enough. It didn't help that one of my headaches was coming on. But for all her flaws and backwards values, my mother really was a kind and loving person. It wouldn't kill me to sit and listen to her for ten minutes. Even if I felt like I was going to die of awkwardness.

"I know this is all going to be new to you. And it's scary. I remember being a little scared, with your father."

I nearly choked. "Mom, please—"

"I want to prepare you. So, my first piece of advice is: it will hurt."

"Listen. I, uh, don't really need to talk about this. I think I've learned everything I need to know from... the internet?" My mom was still under the impression I was a virgin, and I wasn't about to blow my cover now. "So maybe we should just—"

"Just let me say my piece," she interrupted, with a sudden bite in her voice. I glanced at the wooden doors —which she had slid shut, so my father wouldn't hear —and sat back down on the floral upholstered chair.

"Sorry. I just want to prepare you the best way I can," she said, when I'd sat back down. "So, as I said: it will hurt. It will hurt *a lot*. It will hurt so much, he may beg you to stop. But you have to keep going."

I narrowed my eyes at her. "Uh... what? *He's* going to beg me to stop?"

I expected her to correct me and say "you may beg him to stop." But she didn't. Instead, she nodded.

"That brings me to my second piece of advice," she continued. "As you probably know, there may be blood. That's okay, and totally normal. Just ignore it until everything's over. Then it comes off nice and easy with a bit of cold water."

I swallowed. This was getting way too awkward, way too fast. "I actually have a pretty bad headache," I said, getting up. "So maybe we can talk about this later?"

"Oh, speaking of headaches," she said, ignoring my question, "you might get a headache after. That's totally normal too. It's not common, but it does happen."

Sex headaches. I'd gotten them occasionally, and they absolutely sucked. "Okay, what else?" I asked, trying to get this conversation over with as soon as possible.

"You should start before midnight. On the first day of your married life."

"What, that's like, a good luck thing or something?" I asked.

She broke into laughed. Like I'd told the funniest joke she'd ever heard. "You're so funny," she finally said. "Anyway. My last piece of advice is: use this on your lips before the act." And she reached into her pocket and pulled out a small bottle, filled with clear liquid.

Is that lube?! The blood drained from my face. "Okay, uh, I really don't want to talk about this with you anymore," I said, standing up, rubbing my head. "And I'm definitely not going to use... *that*... when we have sex."

She blinked.

"Sex? Why would you use it for sex?" Then, suddenly, she broke into more laughter. "*Oh*, no wonder you're acting so weird. You think I'm talking about sex!"

I stared at her as she laughed, a pit of dread forming in the bottom of my stomach.

"No, dear, I would never talk about that with you! That's your business," she said, waving a hand away. "I'm talking about the ritual of Ka'til."

"... Huh?"

"You know. How us Sampsons have the parasitic crabs Ka'til living in our brains. And how we have to spread it to anyone who officially enters the family. So on your wedding night, you apply this sticky stuff to your lips, make a perfect seal against his mouth, and let some of your crabs crawl into him. He'll be in pain, but it's a necessary evil, you know. I did it with your father, and my father did it with my mother... et cetera." Her lips stretched into a grin. "It's a tradition as old as time."

I stood there, absolutely frozen. My heart pounding in my chest. Feeling the world tilt away from me.

Then I raced out of the room.

My headache was worse now. Way worse. And all I could picture were dozens of tiny crabs, crawling across my brain. Or maybe... *inside* my brain? A wave of nausea hit me and I ran to the bathroom. I threw up, then desperately checked my vomit for crabs. Thankfully, I found none.

Now it's 2 AM and I'm lying awake. Matt has texted me a few times, but I have yet to answer. There's no way I can subject him to this. I just can't do it. My headache is gone, but I almost feel like I can *feel* them, skittering around inside my head. And how many of my thoughts are my own, versus these horrible things?

I know I have to cancel the wedding. But maybe I

can just live with Matt. Maybe he's technically not joining the family that way. Maybe he'll be okay. On the other hand... I should probably just let him go. I love him too much put him in even the slightest amount of danger.

What should I do?

SIGNALING IN THE LAKE

To celebrate our anniversary, my wife and I booked an AirBnB for the weekend–a cabin on the lake. "Looks like it's about to rain," Amber said as she rolled her suitcase across the porch.

I looked up. To the west, the sky was deep gray, thick storm clouds heading towards us at a steady pace. "Just our luck," I grumbled, hauling my suitcase out of the trunk.

After we'd gotten everything inside, we poured wine and sat by the picture window overlooking the lake. The sky was darker, now, and the glassy stillness of the water reflected the deep gray of the sky. The pine trees surrounding the lake swayed in the wind.

"Wait–look," Amber said. "There's someone out there."

At first I didn't see what she was talking about. But then, as I squinted, I did: in the middle of the lake, there was a tiny, peach-colored blob bobbing up and down.

Someone *was* out there.

And they were waving their arms around–as if signaling for help.

"Oh, God, are they drowning?" Amber asked, rushing over to the window.

"Uh, you call the police," I said, getting up and grabbing my jacket. "I'll take the rowboat out and try to help."

The AirBnB had advertised a small rowboat that we could use; I could be out in the middle of the lake in under five minutes. Given how far we were out from town, it would probably take the police twenty minutes to get here.

Amber looked at me, as if she were about to say something; but then she just nodded. I zipped up my coat and ran outside.

The rain had started. A light drizzle blurred the lake in front of me, wetting my face. I ran down to the docks and undid the knot, then stepped into the boat. It rocked violently underneath me as I sat down and pushed off with the oars.

I rowed furiously towards the center of the lake, keeping my eyes on the person. But they were a lot farther out than I had anticipated. Even after rowing five minutes, my arm muscles burning, I was only *slightly* closer.

I stopped for a second and cupped my hands around my mouth. "Hey! I'm coming to help! Hang in there!"

They didn't respond. Just kept waving their arms over their head. *Probably can't hear me,* I thought. Sucking in a deep breath, I began to row faster.

The rain was harder now. Thick raindrops hit the wood of my boat with a *tap-tap-tap*. Water dripped down from my hair and into my eyes. I shook my head to get it off, not breaking stroke, and continued rowing towards the center of the lake.

The person was finally a little closer now. I could see them bobbing up and down on the surface of the lake through the pelting rain, waving their arms furiously above their head. It looked like it was possibly a woman with dark hair, but I couldn't be certain.

The oars sloshed through the lake. I was panting and my arms ached, but I forced myself to continue forward. They weren't that far off now. In just a few minutes I'd probably be close enough to yell out to them, to see them clearly...

Flash.

The sky flashed white. Seconds later–the rumble of thunder, so loud I could feel it in my bones. I swallowed.

This isn't safe.

I glanced back at the cabin. It was so far away, now. I could see the tiny brown blob that was Amber, standing on the docks, waiting for me to return. *Maybe we should've just waited for the police. What if I get struck by lightning?*

I swallowed and turned back to the woman. Paddled as fast as I could with all my might. The rain pelted down furiously, running down my face, pooling in the bottom of the boat. The peach colored blob grew closer and closer, and then–

I could see her clearly for the first time.

Every muscle in my body froze. Because as she

bobbed on the water, waving her hands above her head–

She was smiling.

Not just smiling. Grinning from ear to ear as she stared at my boat approaching. Instinctively I grabbed the oars and backpedaled. The water resisted me, kicking up in loud splashes, and then the boat began to slide away from her–

Riiiiing.

I grabbed the cell phone out of my pocket. It was Amber.

"Drew," she breathed, her voice wavering on the other end of the line. "The police... they said... whatever you do, don't go out into the lake."

"What?"

"Some psycho has been swimming out into the middle of the lake. Luring people out. Just leave her there! Come back–"

She continued talking, but I didn't hear what she said.

Because the woman had disappeared.

The phone fell out of my hands. I grabbed the oars and pulled them towards me, rowing backwards towards the shore as fast as I possibly could. I stared into the water, looking for a ripple, a shadow, anything– but it was impossible. With the rain hitting the surface, the reflections of the storm clouds, there was no way I could tell where she was.

I rowed faster, my heart pounding in my chest. Glancing over my shoulder, I could see that the dock was still so far away. Amber began waving to me, frantically—

Flash.

The sky, the lake, the pine trees at the shore lit up. A peal of thunder rang in my ears. I rowed faster—

And then I heard it.

A *tap-tap-tap.*

From the bottom of my boat.

I didn't have time to react, before the boat flipped over and I plunged into the ice cold water. I broke the surface and gasped in air, screaming, as I grabbed the side of the boat—

Something grabbed my ankle and tugged.

I plunged back into the water. I struggled to pull myself up, but the iron grip on my ankle wouldn't loosen. I kicked and thrashed, trying to pull myself up towards the shadow of the boat above me—

And then the grip released.

I broke the surface, gasping. Then I clawed at the boat, desperately righting it. After a few attempts, I was finally able to get myself back inside. I turned it around and rowed as fast as I possibly could, never looking back.

Miraculously, the woman didn't follow me.

I scrambled up on the dock and Amber hugged me, crying. The police arrived soon after and searched the lake for the woman. But they came up empty-handed. Needless to say, Amber and I cut our trip short. We packed our bags and started the drive home just after the sun had set.

But as we pulled out of the driveway, in the darkness...

I swear I saw a light winking at us, from the middle of the lake.

As if someone was trapped out there, signaling for help.

GOOD LUCK MEANS YOU'LL DIE

I stared down at the D20, tears welling in my eyes.

20.

The fourth one I'd rolled.

Ishaan and Kayla stared at me. Their eyes were wide, filled with fear. I opened my mouth to say something, but I couldn't. Saying it would make it real. And I couldn't—

"It could just be a coincidence," Kayla cut in.

"Yeah, just last week I got two eights in a row," Ishaan said with a nervous laugh.

But we all knew what was really happening.

I'd gotten lucky.

And in this town, getting lucky means you're going to die.

Corey Isenberg was a physics major who lived in an off-campus apartment about a block away from us. Last year—only weeks from graduating—he died in an accident.

"Accident."

His death could have been plucked right out of a *Final Destination* movie. On a bright Monday morning in April, he took the elevator downstairs. Unbeknownst to him, a rat had chewed through the elevator cable that night. As soon as he stepped inside it would snap.

That's not what killed him, though.

Not even close.

He only lived on the second floor. The impact wasn't bad at all. In fact, he was able to press the help button, call the fire department, and calmly tell them that he needed rescue. They dispatched someone, and everything seemed like it would be fine.

But.

Apparently, on the way down, the cable whipped around inside the shaft and got wrapped around a pipe. When the firemen got there, a rather heavyset one stepped on the top of the elevator. It rocked back and forth, pulling the cable taught—

It started spraying water.

Now, I know what you're thinking. Water meets a live wire, and *crack*, he's gone. But nope. The electrical wiring was well insulated. No, what happened was that at that very moment, the fireman started axing through the top of the elevator—and his axe got stuck.

But he'd made a hole.

And the water pouring from the pipe dislodged by

the elevator cable chewed by the rat began to leak into the elevator. *Drip, drip, drip.* The fireman tried to retrieve the axe, but it was stuck. One of the firewomen tried to pry the ceiling off the elevator, but it was sealed very, very well.

In fact, the whole thing was sealed extremely well. So well... none of the water leaking in could leak out.

Corey Isenberg drowned to death inside an elevator.

His death came at the end of an incredible stroke of good luck. I remember reading the headlines in the university newspaper—how he'd won ten grand playing the slots in Atlantic City. There were other things, too, like the time he ran into a tech CEO at Starbucks and ended up getting a job offer. Never would've been there at the right time if his shower hadn't broken earlier that morning.

But his good luck wasn't always so obvious.

It started small—very small. Like the balance in his checking account being $1234.56. Or breaking the wishbone of a chicken exactly in two. Or the random number generator in a line of code popping out three 100's in a row.

Or...

Rolling a die, and getting a natural 20 every time.

I stared at my reflection.

My phone read 2 AM in big fat letters, but I couldn't sleep. Corey's death pounded through my mind. His look of terror as the water level rose. Slamming his fists against the wall of the elevator, screaming for the help that was right on the other side.

But he didn't have a chance.

Fate, luck, chance—whatever you call it—had already marked him to die.

Is that what's going to happen to me?

Corey wasn't the only one. There were several bizarre deaths like this one, spanning across a few decades. In the '90s, Laeta Montgomery burned to death after tripping over a jack-o'-lantern. She'd tripled her wealth at the horse races a week before. In the '00s, Jen Lu was attacked by a rabid squirrel while on a hike with her family. She'd just inherited the entire family business, after her brother announced he'd be moving to England with his fiancee (whom he met in a chance meeting.)

But they might all just be tall tales. None of these details were public—they were passed down from townspeople, from generation to generation. Even with Corey—from news articles I knew he'd died, and that he'd won at the slots, but all the other stuff about wishbones and code was hearsay. Even the details of him drowning in the elevator weren't public. Ishaan told me that.

I shook my head and turned the water on. Splashed some water on my face. *Just a ghost story,* I thought, rubbing the water on my face. *And I'm going to be twenty next month. Aren't I a little old for ghost stories?*

I reached for the towel, to dry my face—

My arm whacked against my phone.

It fell onto the tile with a sickening *crack*. "Dammit!"

I shouted, diving for it. I snatched it off the floor, praying the screen wasn't cracked—

My heart stopped.

The screen was cracked. But it was cracked *perfectly*. One solid line in the glass, running vertically from the bottom to the top. Not a single split or fracture.

Cold sweat broke out on my arms.

I set the phone down, my hand shaking.

I don't know what's going to happen to me. I don't know if I have months or years or days. I don't know if the legend in my town is just a tall tale—snowballing with each generation, as it's told around smoldering campfires on cold autumn nights.

But I don't like my chances.

ALL THE CELLS IN MY BODY ARE DEAD

I should've known something was wrong before the exam. But nothing really jumped out at me. I'm 21 years old, in good shape, with no aches or pains or ailments. Perfect health, really.

There were the little oddities, though. Like the fact that I hadn't needed a haircut in six months. Or the little scratches and scrapes that never seemed to quite heal. I'd even had problems with bugs—sometimes I'd wake up itchy, only to notice several ants crawling up and down my body. Other times I'd notice patches of dusty dirt clinging to my elbows and knees. But I loved the outdoors, and hiked a few times a week, so the bugs and the dirt didn't seem all that strange.

So, I never strung everything together—until I got a biopsy on a suspicious-looking mole.

I knew something was wrong as soon as Dr. Wagner entered the room. After the usual pleasantries, he sat down across from me, a grave look on his face. "We need to discuss the results of your biopsy."

The panic began. *It's melanoma. I have cancer. No no no. I'm only 21—*

"We analyzed the cells, and they did not appear cancerous. However, they were all dead."

"...Huh?"

"All the cells that we analyzed. They weren't abnormal in any way. But they also weren't alive." He pushed out a sigh. "Necrosis can happen for a number of reasons. Frostbite, for example. But I didn't see any signs of frostbite... or anything else that would cause necrosis of skin tissue."

"So what's wrong, then?"

"We need to do more tests," he replied, which I knew was doctor-ese for *I have no fucking idea.*

"What do you *think* it is, though?"

"I'll be honest with you, Cate. I just don't know, at this point." He offered me a forced smile. "But don't worry. Whatever it is, I don't think it's a big deal."

He was wrong.

Dr. Wagner removed the entire mole and sent it to the lab. The analysis came back: all the cells were dead.

Then he took skin samples from a few other areas on my body. They were all dead, too.

"Usually when cells die, including skin cells, they undergo apoptosis," he told me. "As in, they force themselves to implode before they get too old and turn into cancer. But these cells... they're intact. It's just that, the cellular processes aren't happening. It's almost like they're... frozen in time."

"What could cause that?"

A pause. A *long* pause. "Were you exposed to any radiation, or extreme temperatures, or anything else like that recently?"

I shook my head.

"Any recent infections?"

I shook my head, again.

"I'm going to refer you to a rheumatologist. I'd like to rule out autoimmune disease. I also want to refer you to my colleague, Dr. Menendez. He specializes in rare skin conditions."

So he had no idea.

I stared down at my skin, my arms, my feet. They all looked perfectly normal. Healthy, even.

What is wrong with me?

While waiting for my appointments with those doctors, I decided to tell my friend Melanie.

Melanie was one of the smartest people I knew—and she happened to be majoring in biology. It was a long shot that she'd have any ideas, but what else was I going to do? Just stare at the wall, waiting for more inconclusive tests?

"I think we should take a blood sample," Melanie said, after I'd told her everything. And then she pulled the drawer open, riffling through various lab supplies.

"What—*here? Now?*"

She shrugged. "Yeah. Why not?"

"Won't you get in trouble?"

"Nah. Dr. Thompson is really chill about stuff like this."

(As it turned out, Dr. Thompson was *not* really chill about undergrads taking blood samples in her lab, and Melanie almost got kicked out of the school. But that's a whole 'nother story.)

She pricked my finger—which really hurt, actually—but she was nice enough to make conversation to distract me. She asked me about my leave from school six months ago, and if I was feeling better. "Always take care of yourself," she said to me, giving me a pat on the shoulder.

Then she squeezed a drop of blood out onto a slide. She dropped the cover slip on, and the blood instantly expanded into a translucent red pool. She slid it into the microscope and worked at the dials.

"What are you looking for?" I asked, standing awkwardly behind her.

"Stuff."

"Stuff?"

"Just wait."

"Okay."

I waited patiently as Melanie continued to work at the dials, squinting through the microscope.

Then she gasped.

"What—what is it?"

"See for yourself."

I put my eye to the microscope.

I don't really know much about biology. I'm a history major, and I hadn't used a microscope since 9th grade. But I could tell what was going on, sort of: the small reddish blobs floating around were probably red blood cells, and the sea of yellowish liquid was plasma.

"I don't see anything weird."

"Do you see the white blood cells?"

"I have no idea."

She let out a condescending sigh. "The clearish ones?"

I squinted—and then I did see one. It was clear, spotted, and sort of prickly on the edges instead of round. "Yeah, I think so."

"They aren't moving. None of them are." I heard her footsteps on the floor, as she began to pace. "Usually, white blood cells are moving all around, trying to neutralize threats, get rid of infections, that kind of thing. But yours aren't. I think... I think they're dead."

I turned away from the microscope, my heart dropping.

"It makes no sense. If all your white blood cells were dead, *you'd* be dead. You wouldn't be able to fight off the mildest illness or infection. Even the smallest papercut would get infected. But you... you're fine. Alive."

Melanie paced back and forth across the lab, her voice growing excited, frenetic.

"There are so many genetic diseases and disorders we haven't classified yet. So many medical miracles that are still mysteries. What if you're one of them?" She sucked in a breath. "How did life begin? We still don't know, exactly. Can something be alive, while its cells are dead? Before, we didn't think so. But you're sitting there. Alive." She began pacing faster, back and forth, back and forth.

A chill crept down my spine. I didn't like the way Melanie seemed so... excited. So obsessed. I nearly jumped as she stopped pacing and turned to face me, a huge grin on her face.

"We'll show Dr. Thompson. That's what we'll do. We can keep taking samples here, in the lab. Figure out what's going on. It could change the world, Cate. Don't you see? It could change everything we've ever known about life itself."

I got up and, slowly, backed towards the door. "I think I'm gonna go. I have a class early tomorrow."

"No, stay! We have so much to talk about!"

I grabbed the doorknob and ran out.

I expected her to follow me. Maybe chase me down, inject me with horse tranquilizer, and start 'experimenting' on me. But she didn't. When I turned around, the hallway was completely empty.

Every cell in my body is dead.

I've been visiting random doctors, conducting random tests. Covering my tracks by using a different doctor for each test. But everything has come up the same. From cheek cells to skin cells to blood, everything in my body is dead.

It doesn't make sense. My organs are working. My kidneys are still filtering my blood, my eyes are still able to see. My muscles contract and extend as I move around. Yet, no matter what tests I run—biopsies, samples, blood—I don't find a single living cell in my body.

I've been avoiding Melanie. But about three weeks after she took my blood sample, she showed up at my door.

I only answered because I thought she was my grocery delivery. "Melanie," I started. "I'm in the middle of—"

She pushed past me, into my apartment. "I have to tell you something. Please, just, sit."

She looked upset. No longer excited and fascinated by me, but disturbed. I finally sat down, my heart beginning to pound.

"I sent your blood sample to a lab," she breathed, finally sitting down across from me. "They do really in-depth analysis. And I thought—I thought it'd be a good thing, that it would shed light on everything. But... but..." Her voice wavered. She looked like she was about to cry.

"What? What's wrong?"

"They didn't just look at your cells. They looked at the *molecular* makeup of them. The proteins, the molecules, the atoms, the elements, that sort of thing," she said, her voice shaking again. "And it's all wrong, Cate. It's not any of the molecules you'd see in a normal human cell."

"What? What do you mean?"

"It's dirt," she said, her voice shaking. "Dirt and mud and clay. When they ran the mass spectrometer, and analyzed the molecular makeup of your cells, it matched the profile of dirt. Not organic molecules you'd find in a human body."

"What? That's the most ridiculous thing I've ever—"

"Have you ever heard of a golem?" she asked, her voice a high-pitched screech now.

A *golem*. The word sunk into me. Right—the beings in Jewish folklore, made of dirt or clay or other inanimate substance. Animated by God or some other being. Anthropomorphic... but never human. Animated... but never *alive*.

"You're not saying..." I shook my head. "That's crazy. I can't—"

"Six months ago," she said, pulling out her phone. "You, Cate Benson, died of a seizure. Look at the photo. You can't tell me that doesn't look *exactly like you*."

I looked at the article.

All the blood drained out of my face.

There was a photo of me. An obituary. *In loving memory*.

My head swam. I felt weak. Every muscle in my body felt like it had seized up. "You... I don't..."

"Someone couldn't bear to lose you," she said, putting her phone back down on the table. "And this is the way they decided to cope."

I stared down at my hands. At my skin. Made of mud. Made of clay.

Animated, but never alive.

I couldn't believe it. It sounded ridiculous—that I wasn't human, I wasn't alive. I was just an animated mound of dirt. But as I dug deeper, everything began to unravel.

"The obituary says I died a year ago," I whispered, staring at the article. "I don't get it. My leave was only a few weeks—"

"You never took a leave."

I whipped around. "What?"

"I looked you up. You transferred here six months ago. Before that, you were at the University of Delaware," Melanie said, her expression grim.

"What? But I don't remember—"

"When you were created, you were given memories by whoever created you. You're not Cate; her soul wasn't transferred into you, the golem. You were created anew, and whoever made you give you your memories."

"So I can't trust myself. Everything I remember... before six months ago... is wrong, basically."

She nodded.

As she scrolled through forgotten message boards and sites on Jewish folklore, I sifted through my memories. Trying to hang on to anything I could. But the deeper I went, the worse things got. I knew I had a mom and dad—but when I tried to picture them in my head, *really* tried to visualize their faces, I couldn't. I knew stuff about school—I remembered looking in a microscope in ninth grade—but as I replayed the memory in my head, I realized it wasn't my hands turning the knobs of the microscope. They were a shade too dark.

Then I Googled the real Cate Benson. I found her Facebook page, scrolled through photos of friends and family and events. But they were all completely foreign to me. I had no memory of them.

It was just blank.

Melanie and I stayed up all night, trying to find answers. Finally, around 4 AM, she told me she wanted to see my forehead. I awkwardly lifted my bangs as she leaned in, studying my skin.

Then she gasped and led me to the bathroom. "Look!" she said, pointing at my left eyebrow.

There—right above my eyebrow—was a tiny tattoo in white ink. Almost invisible against my pale skin. It read: אמת.

"It's Hebrew for 'truth,'" Melanie said, her voice regaining some of that frenetic, excited energy she'd had in the lab. "Golems have it inscribed on their foreheads, according to folklore. But if someone removes the first letter—the aleph—then it turns into the Hebrew word for 'death.' And then the golem... is deactivated."

I stared at the tiny inscription, my heart plummeting. "So, you mean... if someone removes it... I'll die."

She nodded.

"But no one else knows about the inscription," I said, rearranging my bangs over my forehead.

"No one except your creator."

"Yeah, but my creator wanted me alive. That's why they made me."

"They want you alive, until you're not useful anymore."

My heart plummeted. "What's that supposed to mean?"

"We don't know who created you. It could be your parents, or a friend. But it could be someone else, too." She sucked in a breath. "Who have you been in contact for the past six months?

"I mean... just people here. People who didn't know me before. Some professors, some classmates."

"No one from Delaware? From high school?"

"No." And now that I was seeing it all in retrospect, I realized how strange that was. In six months, I'd never called my parents once. Never made a Facebook or social media account. Never texted a high school friend. All these details, things that should have been jarring to a normal person, had coasted right over me.

"What if they followed you here?" Melanie asked, pacing again. Her bare feet thumped against the carpet. "I mean, it wouldn't make sense to just... make a golem of you, and then disappear. They would've followed you here."

I swallowed.

Hiding in plain sight.

Melanie thought it would be safest for me to leave. I could be on a plane to California tomorrow, leaving whoever created me behind. It would be easy to assume a new identity, considering I was already dead.

But I hesitated. I didn't want to leave the only person who had shown me kindness in my short six months alive—Melanie. And I *liked* it here. I liked the classes. I liked the people. It seemed unfair that I had to be the one to leave.

But my hesitation almost got me killed.

I bought the plane ticket a week in advance. Until then, I tried to live it up. Tried to keep my life on campus as normal as possible. To bury the knowledge that I was an imitation, a *fake,* as deep inside me as I possibly could.

I was walking back home from a dinner when I ran into Jack.

Jack. Why didn't I think of him? I didn't know him well. But we were always running into each other. In the student center, in the dining hall, outside like we were now. Just crossing paths. But it was too often to be just coincidence.

And wait. He mentioned being a transfer student. *Sorry if I'm, like, being too friendly,* I remember him saying, with an apologetic grin. *I'm just new here, and it's so hard to make friends...*

Oh, no, no.

"Hey, Cate!" he said, with his usual grin and a wave. "How have you been?"

"Oh, hey," I said. Trying to keep my tone neutral.

"I feel like I haven't seen you in forever. Where've you been?"

My heart was pounding in my ears. "Uh, just had a lot of homework," I said, backing away. "Sorry, I'm in a rush—can we catch up later?"

"Sure! But hey, can I ask you something real quick?"

I quickened my pace. Away from him. But he jogged

to keep up, to meet me. "I was just wondering if you want to grab dinner tomorrow night. There's this cute little bistro that just opened on Main Street. I thought we could try it out."

"Uh... sure... I guess," I huffed, trying to walk faster. I scanned the campus—but there was no one near us. We were almost at the edge of campus, at my apartment building.

"What's wrong?"

"Nothing. That sounds fine," I replied, my voice too high-pitched.

"You don't want to go with me," he said. And suddenly, his voice was like ice. I glanced at him—and he was staring back at me. Just staring, as he walked with me.

I broke into a run.

My apartment was only a block away. If I could just get there—if I could just—

He grabbed my arm. I reeled back.

"Why are you running from me?" His blue eyes burned into mine.

"Let go of me!"

"You don't want me. You never did." He shook his head and scoffed. "And I thought it would be different this time. I guess I'm just an idiot."

A flash of sliver.

He'd pulled out a pocket knife. He pulled me towards him, yanking my arm—but he wasn't aiming for my throat.

He was aiming for my left eye.

The aleph.

I let out a scream. I tried to wrestle away from him, screaming so loud my own ears hurt. And just as the knife came down—

I heard footsteps.

Two guys were approaching us. "Hey, let her go!" one yelled out.

And then, in an instant, Jack was gone. And I was crumpled on the ground, crying thick, heavy sobs.

I left that night. Melanie and I shared a tearful goodbye at the airport. "Thank you so much, for everything," I told her, as we hugged.

"Of course," she replied, squeezing me back.

As the plane took off into the night, I leaned back in my seat, thinking of the new life I'd start. Of all the things I had yet to experience. Rollercoasters, boyfriends, graduation... it was all before me like the blank pages of an open book.

We can use science to define what's living and what's not. What has a soul and what's simply following the rules of animation. But labels in general can only go so far. Because I know there is something inside me. A spirit, a wisp, *something* that yearns to live.

And I've never felt more alive.

CAUTION: FALLING ROCKS

It appeared on Old Glen Road. A yellow, diamond-shaped hazard sign. No image, just text.

CAUTION: FALLING ROCKS

But the sign wasn't near any rocks. Or any place rocks could fall from. Old Glen Road cut through an expanse of flat woods that went on for miles.

"Meanwhile, there's probably some road next to a cliff with a deer crossing sign," my wife said, when I pointed it out.

"Ha! Well, I hope they fix it soon. It bothers me."

"You could always just, like, roll a boulder on someone. Then the sign would be correct."

"Wow... okay..."

We both laughed and thought the sign would be gone the next day.

But weirdly enough, the sign stayed up through the weeks, then months. I drove past it every morning on my way to work. It became an inside joke between

Rebecca and me: *Leaving now, love you! Bye, honey, watch out for falling rocks!*

Then the accident happened.

It must've happened just a few minutes before I got there. Three police cars were blocking Old Glen Road, lights flashing. And behind them, in the distance... I could make out an enormous rock.

And the crumpled blue metal underneath.

We saw it on the local news channel later that evening. "A car was struck by a falling rock on Old Glen Road this afternoon," the newscaster said. "Paramedics attempted to rescue the driver, Alison Marcetta, but it was too late. She was pronounced dead at the scene."

I didn't know what to say. *How could a rock fall on that road?* It just wasn't possible. It was flat, dense woods as far as the eye could see. A few random houses here and there.

That was it.

"Maybe it's like those magic gravity hills. Like, there's a slope, but it looks like flat land, and then a rock in the woods rolled down and hit her," Rebecca said.

"Maybe."

"Or maybe it was dropped by an animal. Well, not dropped, but kicked or pushed, and then it rolled into the road."

I looked at her. "What kind of animal would be strong enough to move a two-ton boulder?"

She shrugged. "A bear?"

I stared at the TV, showing the same clip of the crushed blue metal under the gigantic rock.

Then I grabbed the remote and switched it off.

"Whatever. I'm taking a different route to work tomorrow."

For the next two weeks, I avoided Old Glen Rd. at all costs. Whatever black magic fuckery was going on there, I didn't want to be a part of it.

But I couldn't ignore it when, again, the local news station was dominated by the story of another victim.

"Local senior George Rodriguez..."

It was the same story. A boulder had fallen from *somewhere* and crushed the poor man on his way to the library.

And the weird thing was, nobody seemed to be talking about it. "You hear about that horrible accident?" I asked my neighbor, when I ran into him getting the mail. "On Old Glen Road?"

"Oh, with the boulder? Terrible. So tragic."

"Yeah, but..."

I hesitated. It seemed kind of disrespectful, in poor taste, for me to start saying how impossible it was. I felt like Roy in that one episode of *IT Crowd*—when he wants to ask his girlfriend how her parents died in a fire at SeaParks, but can't. How could a fire break out when there's water everywhere? How could a boulder roll out and kill someone, *when the land is completely flat?!*

"But what?" Roger looked at me, expectantly.

"How could a rock roll on him? The road, the forest, it's all flat."

He scowled at me. "What are you suggesting?"

"I... I don't know."

He waited for me to say more, but I didn't. What *was* I suggesting? That someone had lifted a boulder and dropped it on the guy's car? That there was some sort of serial killer Hercules on the loose in our town?

"Nevermind," I said, shaking my head.

But later that afternoon, I found myself bored. Rebecca had gone out with some friends, and the house was too quiet for my liking. So I grabbed an old baseball from the attic, got in the car, and set out to Old Glen Road.

The road was quiet and empty when I arrived. No doubt, the reports of the strange accidents had scared people away. I pulled off on the shoulder and stepped out.

I walked into the middle of the street and set the ball down.

It didn't roll.

I walked about fifty feet into the forest on either side and did the same thing. You could blame the leaf litter and uneven terrain for the lack of rolling, I guess. But there didn't seem to be any kind of slope anywhere.

And—to add further to the absurdity of it—I didn't even see any big rocks. I mean, back when I lived in upstate New York, there were rocks *everywhere*. The forests were full of cliffs and boulders and all that stuff. There was a quarry a half-hour away from me, and an old mine.

But here...

Nothing. Just trees and logs and leaves as far as the eye could see.

I glanced back at the sign. Despite the dying light, the letters were clear. **CAUTION: FALLING ROCKS.** I looked up, as if I expected to see a huge boulder sitting there in the tree, but of course there wasn't.

So I began walking back to my car—

And that's when I heard it.

The snap of a twig behind me.

For a second I imagined a huge boulder, rolling towards me through the forest. Indiana Jones-style, leveling trees and flattening birds as it made its fatal descent.

But it wasn't a boulder—it was a person.

A police officer.

"Hello," he called out as he approached.

"Hi," I replied, giving him a tight-lipped smile.

He made his way through the forest to where I was. Only now did I notice the police cruiser parked behind my own car.

"Anything I can help you with?" he asked. He was smiling congenially, but I could tell the question was more of an accusation. *What are you doing out here? Tell me, now.*

"No, I'm just... taking a walk."

"Kind of an odd place to take a walk," he said, as he took a step towards me. "The park's just half a mile down the road."

He was still smiling. But his eyes bored into mine, as if analyzing every detail of my response. "I—well—to tell the truth, I'm scared of dogs," I stuttered. "And that park is overrun with dogs. And quite a few people leave their dogs off their leashes..."

"I see."

Why am I so nervous? I felt hot. Sweaty. The officer's eyes continued to bore into mine—then broke eye contact to look me up and down, taking in every detail. Finally, his ice blue eyes met mine again.

"Well, I regret to inform you that this is private property. You can't be walking here."

"Oh, I didn't see any signs..." I trailed off. "I'm so sorry. I'll leave."

"Thanks," he said, with a sharp nod of his head.

Then he spun on his heel and walked back to the car. As I stumbled back through the forest, I noticed him watching me from behind the tinted glass, his blue eyes tracking my every move.

As soon as I shut the door, I let out a sigh of relief.

He didn't see it.

Before doing all that testing with the baseball, I'd done something crazy. Something Rebecca would chew me out for, if she knew.

I'd tucked a little webcam into one of the trees by the road.

The next accident came only five days later. A young couple, Andrea and John Chen, were killed late last night while driving home from the airport.

My webcam looked like it had caught footage of the crash. One of the clips was timestamped at 11:23 pm—around the right time, according to local news outlets.

Do I really want to watch this?

My cursor hovered over the play button. *Rebecca won't be home until nine thirty. This is your only chance.*

I have to know.

I don't know what I expected to see—but it certainly wasn't what unfolded before me.

The darkness of Old Glen Road, and the surrounding forest, slowly brightened on screen as the car approached. Then white headlights popped into view on the left side of the screen. I held my breath, waiting for the boulder to fall—

CRACK.

The car swerved wildly—then plowed into a nearby tree.

But there was no rock. I squinted at the screen, trying to figure out what had just happened. What caused the sound, caused the car to suddenly crash. But then—

CRACK! CRACK!

The passenger side window shattered.

Gunshots.

I watched in horror as several figures swarmed out of the forest. One still held his gun steady, trained on the car. Another ran to the window, peered in, and then gave some sort of hand signal to the man holding the gun.

I recognized him.

It was the police officer.

Several minutes of commotion. The figures ran around the scene, putting up yellow tape, whispering to each other. Then a great shadow passed over the road, as some sort of truck drove into the frame. No, wait—it was a forklift.

A forklift, *carrying a large boulder*.

I watched in horror as it raised the rock up—and dropped it on the car.

CRUNCH.

My hands shook as I closed out of the video. And then I sat there, stunned, staring at the computer screen.

I don't know how long I sat there. But now, it's almost ten, and Rebecca still isn't home. I know I shouldn't be worried—Rebecca is often late—but I can't help that horrible feeling in the pit of my stomach.

Maybe he did see me put the webcam there.

Maybe he knows.

THE TOWN OF CHELM

I was just getting hungry when I saw the exit.

I could've sworn there weren't exits for a good ten miles along this stretch of 276. But there it was, in big white letters: **43 – Chelm.** As soon as I turned though, I started having doubts; the exit ramp was riddled with cracks and potholes, and the thick pines on either side stretched out into the road, nearly brushing the side of my car.

It looked like no one had been here for a long time.

But when the exit finally merged onto the road, I was pleasantly surprised. A cute little town sat before me: squat offices, a few shops, and a chrome diner. I pulled into the parking lot of the diner and shot off a quick text to my fiancee, Reena. **Hey, sorry, gonna be home later than I thought. Getting dinner in Chelm, which is about two hours away, I think.**

Her text popped up almost immediately. **Chelm? Like the wise men of Chelm?**

I don't know what that is, I replied.

It's a Jewish thing. Like little folktales and jokes about the dumb things people do in this fictional town called Chelm. My grandpa used to tell me a lot of them.

Oh that's cool! I replied, before slipping the phone in my pocket and making my way across the parking lot.

Bells chimed above my head as I entered the diner. It was fairly crowded, but I found a booth in the back next to an elderly couple. A pretty young waitress swung by and dropped off a menu. I opened it up, but nothing jumped out at me. It seemed like standard diner fare: omelets, turkey sandwiches, chicken noodle soup.

"What can I get for you?"

"Uh..." I glanced at the waitress, then back at the menu, and frowned. I was really in the mood for something totally decadent, like chicken-fried steak, but I hadn't seen it on the menu. "Can you do chicken-fried steak?"

"Let me check with the chef."

She hustled away and I looked back at my phone. Reena hadn't texted me further, so I aimlessly scrolled through the news. I was reading about some story of a huge swordfish caught off the coast of Florida when—

"Excuse me, sir?"

I looked up at the waitress. She was frowning. "I'm sorry," she said, "but chickens don't know how to fry steak."

I blinked. "... What?"

"You asked for chicken-fried steak. But chickens

can't fry steak. They're too dumb. Would you like human-fried steak instead?"

"Uh..." I let out an awkward laugh. But she wasn't laughing—she wasn't even smiling. "I'll just get a veggie omelet," I said uneasily, handing her the menu. "With buttered toast. Is that good?"

"Yes! I'll get that for you right away."

She turned around and headed for the kitchen doors. I shook my head. *What a weird interaction.* I took a sip of my water and reached for my phone, finishing the article about the swordfish.

The waitress came back fifteen minutes later with the omelet. As I reached for the fork, though, I accidentally knocked one of the pieces of toast to the floor. "Oh, *fuck*," I muttered.

A loud gasp. I looked up to see the waitress standing there, eyes wide. "Oh, sorry, I didn't mean to—"

"Look at the *toast*," she whispered, her lip trembling.

My heart dropped. She sounded so fearful. I looked down, not knowing what to expect. Maybe one of those things where the pattern of browned bread looks like an angel or a demon or something. But all I saw was a normal piece of toast, sitting on the carpet.

"Uh... I don't... what?"

"It landed *butter-side up!*"

And at that, the entire diner was thrown into pandemonium.

The old man next to me whipped around. Jumped out of his booth. "Margaret!" he shouted, motioning to his wife. "Margaret, *look!*"

I watched, stunned, as every single person in the

diner got up, ran over, and swarmed around the toast. Including the staff—the busboys, the waiters, the waitresses, the chef. *"How is that possible?!" "I've never seen toast land butter side up." "It's an omen of the end times!" "DON'T TOUCH IT JIMMY!"*

What... the fuck?

If this whole thing were a scene in a sitcom, it would be hilarious. But actually seeing it happen in real life... it was horrifying. *This isn't how normal people act.*

There is something seriously wrong here.

"We must consult Rabbi Blau," the chef finally announced, rushing back towards the kitchen.

I expected the crowd to dissipate. But it didn't. The dozen or so diner patrons remained circled around me, staring in horror at the piece of toast.

Okay, fuck it. This is too weird. I reached into my pocket, pulled out a twenty, and threw it on the table. *I don't know what the hell is wrong with these people, but I'm not staying to find out.*

I got up and started for the door—

A hand grabbed me. Pulled me back.

I wheeled around. It was the old man. He held my wrist in a vice grip, and his cold blue eyes bore into mine. "Where are you going?"

"Uh—I've got to get home. My girlfriend's waiting for me—"

"Don't you want to hear what Rabbi Blau says?"

"... About the toast?"

He nodded, solemnly.

What the fuck is wrong with these people?! I yanked my

hand out of his grip. "Sorry, I have to go," I said as I rushed towards the door—

"It's my fault!"

I turned to see the chef rushing out of the kitchen. "Rabbi Blau explained it perfectly. The reason why the toast fell butter-side up, instead of butter-side down, is because *I buttered it on the wrong side!*"

Understanding *"oh"*s and *"ah"*s filled the room like a chorus. People smiled, nodding approvingly. Then, slowly, they made their way back to their own tables. The chef picked the toast up off the floor and gave me a smile. "I'll just butter this on the right side for you, and bring it back, okay?"

"Actually... I'm gonna go," I said, backing towards the door.

As soon as the chef disappeared back in the kitchen, I swung the door open and hightailed it to the parking lot.

What is wrong with these people?! It was like they didn't understand basic logic. Like they were aliens from another planet, trying to act the way they thought people acted. *Who cares that much about a piece of toast? And buttering it on the wrong side? That doesn't even make sense. The sides are identical until it's buttered.*

I sprinted across the parking lot towards my car—

And stopped dead.

No. No, no, no.

My tires were slashed.

The blood drained out of my face. I stood there, frozen, my heart pounding in my ears. *They slashed my tires. They're trapping me here. What... the...*

My thoughts trailed off. I suddenly felt that horrible, nagging feeling in my chest. The hairs on the back of my neck prickled.

And I knew—I was being watched.

I whipped around. The people in the diner... they had their faces pressed against the glass.

Every eye on me.

Fuck. I gotta get out of here.

My first thought was to get in the car. Until I noticed that all that remained of the windows was some shattered glass, clinging to the frame. I began to panic.

Calm down. You still got your phone. I'd call the cops, and hope I could stay hidden until they arrived. I darted into the row of bushes that separated the parking lot from the street, frantically dialing 911.

"911, what's your emergency?"

"Hi. I'm... I'm in Chelm. At Ruth's Diner. And the people, they slashed my tires, I think they want to do something horrible and—"

"Slow down," the operator replied. "I can barely understand you."

"I'm at Ruth's Diner. I can't leave because someone slashed my tires."

"Would you like tape?"

My stomach dropped. "I... what?"

"Would you like some tape to repair your tires?"

A sick feeling washed over me. "Who... who is this?" I stuttered.

"Chelm Police Department!" the voice on the other end said cheerily.

I hung up the phone. Peering through the branches,

I saw that the people were slowly exiting the diner and starting to follow me. I darted out of the bushes and broke into a sprint.

After a couple of zig-zagging turns, I found myself on a residential street. Thankfully, it seemed like I'd lost the diner people. At least for the moment. I came to a stop, panting.

And that's when I realized that the weirdness of Chelm didn't stop at the diner.

In the front yard of one house, a man was digging an enormous hole. "Those airfares are too expensive," he yelled to his wife. "This is the cheapest way to get to China!" Across from me, a woman was watering her petunias with a teaspoon. And there was a child, struggling to ride a bicycle with square-shaped wheels.

What... the...

But I didn't have much time to think about it. The slapping of feet against pavement sounded behind me —and I turned to see the people from the diner, running down the street at top speeds.

"Get him!" one of them screamed.

Immediately, the man stopped digging. The woman dropped her teaspoon. Even the child launched off her bicycle and started towards me.

No, no, no—

Someone grabbed me.

I turned to see an old lady pulling me by arm. "Get—get off me!" I screamed.

"Shut up," she muttered. "I'm trying to save you from these fools."

There was something about her voice. Her eye contact. That made me believe her.

I sprinted down the street until she yanked me towards a little brick house. She swung the door open and pulled me inside. Then she quickly moved behind me, drawing a series of deadbolts and locks. Afterwards she brought her fingers to her lips, kissed them, and quickly touched the mezuzah next to the front door.

"You're safe in here," the woman said, brushing past me into the living room.

I glanced around. Trash bags were taped over the windows, blocking out almost all the daylight. The house was lit with a single chandelier in the dining room, casting long shadows across the carpet. I followed her and took a seat in one of the chairs, my legs weak from running.

"What's... what's wrong with them?"

"Oh, my boy. Everything. Everything is wrong with them." She sunk down in the armchair across from me. The deep shadows cast by the chandelier cut into her wrinkles, making her appear decades older. "It happened about ten years ago. There was a bad storm. Lots of lightning, thunder. I happened to be in the basement the entire time, doing the laundry. And I think, somehow... that's what saved me.

"When I came up from the basement, my husband Richard was in the kitchen. But he was just... standing there... staring out the window. The first couple times I called his name, he didn't even respond. Finally, he did. But within a few minutes, I knew there was something horribly wrong with him.

"I can't quite describe it. It was like something had taken away his common sense. His intellect. He would obsess over the strangest things. One day he went fishing. The fish put up quite a fight, and ended up slapping him right in the face. He was really angry, so he went to Mayor Goldman. She sentenced the fish to death by drowning for its assault on my husband. So they went to the lake together, rowed out into the very center, and dropped the fish in. Does that make any sense to you?"

I shook my head.

"The man I married... he was gone. As were most of the people in the town."

"Why don't you leave?"

"Because I'm trying to find a cure." She glanced up at the fireplace mantle, which held several photos of her and Richard. "It's not just me. There are a couple people here, who weren't affected. We've all lost loved ones, and we're trying to find a way to cure them. We haven't been successful so far, but..." She shrugged. "I can't give up on Richard."

"And the others... they don't come after you?"

"No. When I go out, I act like one of them. I keep the windows covered so they don't see me acting normal. It's what we all do. And it works. Pretty easy to fool a town of fools, I suppose," she said, with a forced smile that didn't meet her eyes. "Anyway. You'll be able to leave in a few hours. They all go to bed at precisely the same time—ten o'clock. Then it's safe to move around freely. I'll call you a cab, but you'll have to walk a bit out of town, so you don't draw attention to yourself."

"What about my car?"

"Sorry. Unless you want to risk waking them up and finding you... you'd probably better leave it."

I paled. I couldn't afford to lose my car. Then again, I couldn't exactly afford to get mauled by these strange people.

Get out of here first. Tomorrow, you can go down with the police and try to retrieve it.

I walked out of town in the darkness, and made about a mile up the desolate road. The cab pulled up near eleven, and I almost expected it to be driven by one of the fools. But it was just some random guy who chewed his gum too loudly.

He dropped me safely back home, and I relayed the whole story to Reena. She didn't believe me at first, thinking it was all an elaborate prank on my part. Then she thought maybe the entire town was pranking *me*, based on the stories of Chelm. Or maybe it was some sort of flash mob or social experiment.

I had to agree with her—those stories seemed more likely than the woman's explanation about the storm.

But the next morning, when I called the police and tried to retrieve my car, I found that there wasn't an exit 43 on route 276. It was just a blank stretch of highway. All I could see were thick pines and tangled bushes where the exit ramp had curved off.

It was like the town of Chelm never even existed.

VOICES IN THE WOODS

There's a stream in the woods behind my house. And for some reason, that stream is a homing beacon for any young man in a hundred-mile radius. I hear them drunkenly shouting into the wee hours almost every weekend. Skinny-dipping, taking drugs, who knows.

Tonight was no different.

"Yo! Incoming!" *Splash.*

"You little fucker!"

Despite the stupidity of their conversation, a chill ran down my back. Who knows what a few drunk—and possibly high—guys would do if they knew a 25-year-old woman was living all alone, just a few hundred feet from the stream.

Splash!

"You *fucker!* I'm going to kill you!"

"Ahahaha!"

Wild laughs rang out through the forest.

I paced into the darkened great room. *Front door*

locked. I continued through the kitchen, to the back door. *Locked.* Opened the garage. *Yep, locked.* Brecia looked up at me sadly from her dog bed, and gave a whine.

"You're a tired little fluffball, aren't you?"

I glanced at the clock. 12:21 AM. The drunken whooping continued. It sounded louder. Or was it my imagination?

Only a few hours until dawn, I told myself.

I padded back into the great room, sat in the rocking chair, and picked up my book. The wood creaked underneath me as I rocked. I began to read. *To build an effective compost pile, you must have the proper balance of nitrogen and carbon. Otherwise, you risk—*

"Hey guess what? *Emily* looked real good last night."

You must have the proper balance of nitrogen and—

"Did she laugh at your tiny dick?"

"Ooooh! *BUUURRN!*"

I snapped the book shut. Crossed my arms. Laughter rang out, and more whooping. The chair creaked underneath me. The voices seemed to grow louder as I sat there, fidgeting madly, rocking faster and—

Brecia started growling.

A low growl, emanating through the entire house. I shot up from the chair, my heart pounding, and ran into the kitchen.

She wasn't in the dog bed. She was standing at the sliding glass door, peering through the hanging blinds. Hackles raised. Growling.

Heart hammering, I walked over to the door. Parted

the blinds, peered out into the woods. Couldn't see a damn thing. It was a moonless night.

The voices continued.

"Come on, man, this is fucking lame."

"Yeah, let's go up that way."

No, please no...

Footsteps. Snapping branches. Their voices continued, growing louder by the second.

And then I heard four words that made my heart jump.

"Hey, who's that woman?"

They can see me. Shit, shit, shit. I jumped away from the door, letting the blinds fall with a clatter. Brecia growled.

"Hey, lady! Do you need help?"

...Huh?

Then hushed tones, barely reaching my ears through the woods.

"Why is she just lying there?"

"Is she dead?"

I stood there, my brain racing to catch up.

"Let's get the fuck out of here."

"Wait! We gotta call someone! We can't just *leave* her there!"

I stood at the door, my body frozen. I couldn't move. Couldn't speak. *They found a body?* I backed away, further into the kitchen. Brecia growled again.

And then the voices changed.

"Wait, she's moving!"

"Call 911!"

"Do you need he—"

The voices cut off.

And then the screams started.

Horrible screams. The heart-wrenching, awful screams of someone in absolute agony. I grabbed my phone and dialed 911.

But by the time the operator picked up, there was only silence.

PHOTOS OF ME SLEEPING

My stepdaughter has been taking photos of me while I sleep
posted by B___ on August 28, 2023

I don't know what to do. I'm really freaking out right now. Apparently, my stepdaughter has been taking photos of me while I sleep. I could really use some help.

To back up: six months ago, I married my husband, who we'll call "Harry." Harry has a daughter from a previous marriage (13F), "Lily." I don't have kids. Lily and I have never gotten along. However, in the past few months—since we got married—things have gotten much worse.

She used to just ignore me. Now, she's actively aggressive. I found paint on my favorite heels. She "accidentally" used one of my favorite T-shirts as a cleaning rag. She even spilled some sort of black ink in our bed during an art project or something like that, who knows.

Harry's talked to her. Over and over again. But he hasn't really *disciplined* her. I keep telling him she needs to see the consequences of her actions, but he's too much of a softie to actually ground her, or take away her phone, etc. "She's going through a tough time," he keeps telling me. "Please, just let her be for a few months."

I tried to ignore it. But then it got worse.

Harry was on a three-day business trip, so I was completely in charge of Lily. And she amped it up to 11. The very first morning, she came down the stairs wearing one of my necklaces.

"You can wear my jewelry, but need to ask me for permission first," I told her.

"I don't need to ask permission for *anything*," she replied, rolling her eyes.

"Yes, you do. For the next three days, your dad's gone, so you need to listen to me."

"No, I don't! You're not my mom!" she shouted.

Then she pulled at the necklace—and snapped it right in two.

I wanted to scream. But instead, I calmly confiscated her phone.

Harry would be furious with me. But I'd had enough. When she got home from school, she ran into her room and locked the door, crying. I explained everything to Harry over the phone. I could hear the annoyance in his voice, but he agreed that she needed to learn, and it was okay to keep her phone for a few days.

So I thought things were looking up.

Then it happened.

Later that night, after Lily went to bed, I wanted to take a picture of our cat. But I grabbed Lily's phone by mistake. And after I took the photo, when I went to the camera reel—

I found a photo of myself.

Sleeping.

What. The. Fuck.

It was a dark, grainy photo. She hadn't used the flash. But I could still make out my face, clearly, smushed against the pillow. Eyes closed. I could make out Harry's silhouette in the background behind me, facing the other way, and my book on the nightstand.

Before I could stop myself, I flipped to the next photo.

And there was another one. Another one of me sleeping. Taken from a different angle.

Taken from below.

Like she'd been hiding under the bed.

Fuck. Fuck, fuck, fuck. My thumb raced across the screen as I flipped back through the photos. There were *dozens* of them. Dozens of photos of me sleeping. One taken from inside our bathroom. Another taken from inside our *fucking closet*. I looked at the timestamp on them—they were all taken around 2 AM. Over the course of *weeks*.

I tried to call Harry. Three times. But his phone went right to voicemail. It was after midnight, and he had an early meeting tomorrow. He must've turned it off.

"Come on, come on…" I muttered, calling him a fourth time.

"Jen?"

I jumped about a foot in the air.

Lily was standing behind me. In the semi-darkness. Her wavy hair hung halfway over her face. I backed away. "What do you want?" I asked, quickly ending the call.

"I want my phone back."

"Not—tonight," I replied, my heart pounding. "Maybe tomorrow."

She shrugged. "Okay."

Then she went back upstairs and into her room.

I flipped through the photos one more time. Why in the world would she take these photos? To intimidate me? To scare me? To help her plan of murdering me?

Or…

There was a much more likely, much less sinister reason. She could've taken them to embarrass me. Maybe she planned to post them all over TikTok or Instagram. Me, sleeping with my mouth open, looking like shit.

Really mean of her.

But not psychopathic.

Still, I locked my door that night anyway.

After talking to Harry, I felt better. He thought the same thing—she was taking them to post them online or something—but he was now in total agreement with me. "This has gotten out of hand. I'm gonna talk to her as soon as I get back."

So that was a relief, at least.

"Can I have my phone back today?" Lily asked, when I picked her up from school.

"If you're really, *really* nice, I'll give it back. Okay?" I'd just lock the bedroom door at night. She couldn't take more photos of me.

But later that night, I regretted my promise.

Lily was a model kid. She thanked me for dinner. She washed her dishes. She even folded the towels sitting on the dryer! And while I didn't want to give the phone back, I wanted to reward her for being so good.

So I gave it back.

At 2:30 AM I woke with a start.

As I sat up in the darkness, I realized what woke me up. A clicking, metallic noise. It was coming from the door.

Just as I started to get out of bed—the door creaked open. And there was Lily, with a bobby pin in her hands.

She'd picked the lock.

"What are you doing?!" I hissed.

Her eyes went wide. Then she ran back down the hallway, towards her room. I jumped out of bed, running after her. "Hey! HEY!" I shouted. "Why are you taking pictures of me?! *Why?!*"

She stopped. Then, slowly, she turned around.

"Dad didn't believe me. So I had to take the pictures."

"Didn't believe you? About what?"

She didn't say anything. Instead, she handed me her phone. She swiped to the first photo of me, taken in the darkness. Grainy and dark. She pointed to the ceiling. "Look."

"… At what?"

"Turn the brightness up."

I did—and then I gasped.

There was something there. On the ceiling. Spindly long shapes crisscrossing each other. Even with the brightness turned way up, it was hard to make out; but there was definitely something there.

She flipped to the next photo.

And the next.

My heart began to pound. It was like watching one of those old flipbook animations. In slow motion, with each swipe, the *thing* on the ceiling unfolded itself.

And began reaching for the bed.

I stared at the final photo. The one she'd just taken, minutes ago. Me sitting up in bed, my face twisted in anger and shock as I cried out for Lily.

And behind me—long, spindly arms reaching for me.

The phone fell out of my hands.

"Dad didn't believe me. When I showed him the pictures, he didn't see it. He yelled at me and said I was reading too many scary stories. So I've been showing them to my friends. We've been trying to figure out what it is… but we don't know."

Lily and I are staying at a friend's place for the time

being. We're not going back there. Not until we talk to Harry, not until we figure this out. Does anyone know what this could be? We've been searching nonstop and haven't found anything promising.

AFTERIMAGE

It first happened at Zoey's birthday party.

The three of us posed for a picture. The phone flashed brightly in our eyes, lighting up the dark bar. And when I looked away, briefly—

There was something wrong with the afterimage.

There was the usual sort of shimmery brightness, floating in front of my vision. But in the center... there was a hole, or a darkened blob, or something. With a flash from a photo, it should've just been a uniform, shimmery circle... but it wasn't.

It only lasted for a second, then faded away. I was back to staring at my friends' smiling faces, the two men leering at us at the end of the bar, and the bright-pink drink in front of me.

So I forgot about it.

Until I was on my phone the next night. As usual, I was staying up way later than I should, doomscrolling through social media updates that made everyone else's lives look perfect. When I finally turned my phone off a little before 1 am and closed my eyes, I saw the perfect imprint of the screen against the back of my eyelids, shimmering and glittering like stars.

Except there was a blob in the middle.

Since my eyes were closed this time, I could see it a little more clearly. The edges were blurry, as all afterimages are, but it almost looked like... a man?

Like a little man, standing there on the backs of my eyelids.

I frowned. *Had I been looking at a photo of a man?* I tried to think about what I'd looked at before I turned off the phone. *I had been looking at photos... of Jesse's baby shower, of Josh's hike in the Appalachians...*

I shrugged. The last photo must've had a man in dark clothing, standing in the middle of a bright background. Or something like that.

The afterimage faded and I drifted off to sleep.

Weeks went by and I never even thought about the afterimages. But then, one night, I was scrolling through Reddit posts, wasting time. And on one of those subreddits, like damnthatsinteresting or blackmagicfuckery or something like that, they had an optical illusion. There was a black-and-white drawing of a woman's face, with a red dot on her nose. Supposedly, if you stared at the red dot for 30 seconds and then looked at a blank wall, you'd see her image on the wall.

I'd done optical illusions like this as a kid. Still, I had

nothing better to do, so I went ahead and stared at the red dot for 30 seconds.

1... 2... 3...

Damn, this was harder than I remembered.

11... 12... 13...

My eyes were tearing up a little. I blinked.

28... 29... 30.

I looked at the wall—

And froze.

I saw the woman's face. But there, slightly off-center—under her left eye—was the *clear* silhouette of a man.

I just stared, until the shimmering lines of the afterimage faded away. Until the wall was blank white, like it was supposed to be. I took a deep breath, walked over to the kitchen, splashed water on my face.

What the fuck was that?

No no no. That must be part of the illusion. I scanned the comments, looking for mention of a man. But there were only three (it was a new post) and they were perfectly ambiguous. Just saying things like '*wow, so cool!*'

I turned off the phone, slid it away from me, and hid my head in my hands.

I *really* needed to cut down on my screen time.

I used to play a game when I was little.

When I couldn't sleep, I'd rub my eyes for a long time. It would create this strange pattern of colors and shapes, blooming over the inside of my eyelids, and my brain would turn it into a story. A movie playing before my eyes. Pareidolia—our brain's ability to see faces in knots of wood, or see sheep and birds in fluffy white clouds—is a powerful thing.

I'd see strange patterns of colors that looked like weird lanscapes from a Dr. Seuss book. I'd see blobby shapes that looked like little fantastical critters scampering about. But weirdly, they'd all end the same way. Around ten minutes in or so, I'd see an annulus of shimmering color, surrounding a big circle of nothingness.

Almost like a ginormous eye, staring back at me.

I hadn't done it in years. But here I was now, ready to start: lying in bed, eyes closed, hands raised. I was having trouble sleeping, and it occurred to me: if there really was this man I kept seeing, shouldn't I see him when I close my eyes?

I began to rub my eyes. The colors bloomed before me, inside my eyelids. Vivid reds spiraled around each other. Sparkling darkness chased them back, ate them away. A psychadelic vortex replaced them, made of bubbling circles that reminded me of a Julia fractal. The pattern looked like something out of an LSD trip, a vortex pulsing with my own heartbeat.

And then—

A dot of darkness, at the center of my vision.

I continued rubbing my eyes, and the darkness grew. But it wasn't the shimmery, sparkling darkness that appeared in the patterns. It was just... the absence of everything. As it grew, it looked more and more out of place; an empty void next to shimmering, dancing colors.

And then I saw it clearly.

It was the shape of a man.

A tall, thin man with arms that hung limply at his sides. A neck slightly too long, a gaunt stretched face. A complete absence of color. The silhouette grew in my vision, slowly, cutting through the shimmering colors.

He's getting closer.

And then he moved. A long, spindly arm slowly lifted up, stretching towards me, reaching out for me—

My eyes snapped open.

I stared up at the white ceiling. For a second—just the briefest, most fleeting moment—I saw his afterimage, projected onto the blank ceiling.

And then nothing.

I don't know how long I lay there, panting, my entire body seized up like I couldn't move. Then, finally, I turned on the lights and called a friend, who I told the entire story to, start to finish.

And now I'm here, on Reddit, posting about it to strangers.

Because I don't know what to do. I've gone down every rabbit hole on Google. I've even seen an ophthalmologist. I've never been a superstitious person, but it's hard for me to believe that what I saw is just something wrong with my eyes.

I think it's something far, far worse.

OCD

I have OCD. Every night, before I go to sleep, I check things.

I check the refrigerator, from top to bottom. There can't be any candy or other tempting things on the top shelf, because my kids could climb on the shelves and topple the fridge on themselves and die. But there can't be any dangerous things on the lower shelves, like plastic produce bags, because they could suffocate on those.

I check all 12 outlets downstairs. Each one has to be covered with an outlet cover. There also can't be anything plugged in, because that could cause a fire at night. And my kids could strangle on them.

I remove all cups of water. Things can fall in them overnight. They get dirty. If the kids drink a cup left out overnight, they could choke or get sick. The only cup of water I leave out is one by my 5 year old's bedside, in case he gets thirsty in the middle of the night. I shine a flashlight in it and check it before I go to sleep.

I check all the knives. They can't be in the dishwasher because my kids could get them. They can't be in the drawer either. They can't be in a cabinet, though, because they could fall on someone. I usually push them to the very back of the cabinet, behind something, so they can't fall.

And then I take a photo.

That's right. I take a photo of every single thing I mentioned, plus about twenty other things. If you scrolled through my phone right now, 90% of the photos would be locked doors, baby gates, outlets, knives...

Does this sound exhausting? It is. The whole process takes me about an hour. My husband thinks it's a huge waste of time.

But apparently, I'm not doing enough. Because Friday morning, I woke up to find one of the knives out.

Well, it wasn't "out." But it was in the middle of the cabinet shelf, instead of pushed behind the cereal boxes. That was *not* where I left it.

"Evan! Did you move the knives?!"

He poked his head out of the family room. "No. Why?"

"It's not in the right place."

I checked the knives last night. I knew I did. And yet... when I checked the photos on my phone, there wasn't a photo of the knives.

Did I actually forget?

I *was* sleep-deprived. My 2-year-old had been

waking up consistently at 5 AM this week. Maybe I really had just forgotten.

Over the next few days, though, more weird things happened. For example—I have two baby locks on the closet door. I always lock both, so that if one fails the kids still can't get in. On Monday morning, however, I found one of them unlocked.

Just one.

Which was weird, because if someone had opened the closet and forgotten to lock it... *both* would be unlocked.

On Tuesday morning, I found a pudding cup on the top shelf of the fridge. There were also other things out of place in the fridge. Looked like someone had gone through the entire fridge, messing everything up.

But, again, I couldn't be sure, because the photo was missing.

On Wednesday morning, I found the attic door ajar. "Evan!" I shouted. "Do *not* leave the attic door open!" A few years ago we had bats up there. We hadn't been up there since then, and it was likely there were more bats. With rabies. We were all going to get rabies because my husband couldn't follow a simple set of rules.

But Evan just shook his head. "I haven't been up in the attic," he said, shrugging.

And then there was Thursday.

On Thursday morning, I found a single outlet cover missing from the living room.

No one even uses that outlet. It's in an awkward place by the front door. It made no sense for it to be missing.

I grabbed my phone and scrolled back through the photos. But the photo of the outlet was gone. Just like the photo of the knife and the closet and the fridge and the attic.

Had I really forgotten to check those things? My OCD is pretty severe. The last time I forgot to check something on the list was when I had COVID. And it only happened once—not so many days in a row.

"Is something wrong?" Evan asked, as we made breakfast.

"Huh?"

"You're so quiet. Is everything okay?"

"Yeah, I..." I trailed off. "Just so tired lately."

"I'm sorry." He wrapped his arms around me. "I love you. See you tonight, okay?"

That night, I spent almost an hour and a half checking things. I took more than sixty photos, and then I reviewed them, making sure I'd checked everything on my list. I wouldn't sleep otherwise. By the time I got in bed, it was almost midnight, and Evan was already asleep.

I knew I'd done a good job.

Which is why I nearly fainted when I found a cup of water on the kitchen table.

It was just sitting there. In the dead center of the table. In a plastic Hulk cup I didn't even remember using yesterday.

I stood there. Frozen. My heart pounding in my chest.

I checked everything last night.

There's no way.

No way.

Unless my son got it in the middle of the night? But he's too short to use the faucet without the stepping stool. (Which I keep in the closet because if it's out he could stand on it, topple into the sink, and drown.)

I searched through my photos. Technically, I hadn't taken a photo of the kitchen table itself. But still... I'm sure I checked for cups and dumped them all. *I'm sure.*

That night, I checked things even more thoroughly. Exhausted, I fell asleep as soon as my head hit the pillow.

Something woke me with a start.

I looked at my phone. 1 AM. I rolled over—and then I froze.

I heard footsteps downstairs.

Slow, methodical footsteps, traveling through the house. And then the realization hit me. All the pieces came together in horrible clarity in my head. *Oh God. What if... someone's been living in the house?*

Living in the attic?

Moving our things? Eating our food?

I held my breath, my heart pounding in my ears. It was crazy, but—it made sense. The attic, slightly open... what if someone was living up there? We hadn't been up there in years. What if they were coming downstairs while we slept, eating food from our fridge, drinking out of our cups, maybe even plugging in their phone to charge?

"Evan—"

My breath caught in my throat.

He wasn't in bed.

I scanned the dark room. The door to our bedroom hung slightly ajar. "Evan?" I whispered. No response.

I forced myself out of bed and stepped out into the dark hallway. No one there. Then I crept down the stairs, going as slowly as possible so the wood wouldn't creak.

Then I saw him—and all the blood drained out of my face.

Evan was crouched in the living room.

Crouched over an outlet.

My hand clapped over my mouth. I stared, in horror, as he removed the outlet cover. As it clattered to the floor. As he picked it up and slipped it into his pocket.

I backed up the stairs. Praying he wouldn't see me. I ducked into the bedroom and pulled the covers over me, my heart pounding.

Evan...

It's him.

What kind of fucked-up game is he playing?

His shadowy silhouette stepped into the doorway. The bed creaked as he joined me in bed. I held my breath, staring at the wall, heart pounding in my chest. Motion appeared in my vision and I flinched—but he was only reaching over me, taking my phone off the nightstand.

I watched over his shoulder as he selected my photo of the outlet—and then deleted it.

I heard a soft laugh escape from his lips.

Then he put my phone back on the nightstand, rolled over, and went to sleep.

It's nearly dawn now. I haven't slept a wink with

that monster sleeping next to me. I've just been staring at the wall, trying to form a plan.

Trying to figure out how to get away from him in one piece.

Because whatever fucked-up game he's playing here—

I know it doesn't end well for me.

I VISIT MY DEAD MOTHER EVERY NIGHT

My mom died ten years ago.

Not a day has gone by where I don't think about her. How much I miss her. Or a funny thing I would've shared with her, if she were still alive. All those hypothetical questions that come up, like "if you had a genie, what would you wish for?" or "who would you choose to have dinner with, living or dead?," I answered the same way: my mom.

And then, one day, those questions became reality.

I read some urban legend online. It was stupid, but I was a gullible 24-year-old coming off a break up, and admittedly a little drunk. So on a lonely Friday night, I found this post on a dusty old message board:

If you go to the corner of Maple Ave. and Willow St. in [REDACTED], OH at exactly midnight, you will find a ticket dispenser. There is a numeric keypad on it and a big red button. Enter the date you would like to visit on the keypad

(MM/DD/YYYY) *and then press the big red button. Take the ticket that comes out.*

There were more instructions that I skimmed over. I had to be holding the ticket, or have it in my pocket, and open a door (any door!) at exactly midnight. If I did all off that, supposedly, I would be transported back to that day.

I didn't actually expect it to work. But the next day, when I was sober, I drove to the corner at exactly midnight. And there, gleaming under the streetlight, was an old ticket dispenser.

It looked like the kind you see in parking garages. Or maybe the kind train stations had, before everything became digital. Just a little metal box with a keypad and a red button. I pulled over, got out of the car, and walked up to it.

I typed in 02/24/2007—my eighth birthday. It wasn't some epic day of parties; I was having a party on the weekend. But my parents still wanted to make my actual birthday special, so they took me to see Eragon and get ice cream with them on my real birthday. It was a fun day —just the three of us, enjoying each other's company, my parents making dumb jokes about the movie and eating an enormous serving of Rocky Road. Then reading a bedtime story, checking for the monster in the closet I was always going on about, and tucking me in.

The keys clicked under my fingers. A mechanical whir pierced the silence. And then the ticket pushed out of the slot. It was pretty nondescript: a white ticket with the words "ROUND TRIP, 02/24/2007" printed on it, along with a small symbol or emblem printed in gold ink.

I got greedy. I tried a few more times, entering a few other dates that stood out in my mind. After three tickets, however, the machine only made an angry mechanical sound.

I guess three was the limit.

And so, at midnight the next night, I decided to give the first one a try.

I was skeptical. But I'd come this far on this stupid journey, might as well try it. The ticket was securely tucked away in my pocket, and one hand was on the doorknob, the other holding up my phone. I stared at the clock, waiting for the instant that 11:59 turned to 12:00.

I turned the doorknob.

No way.

There was a staircase inside my closet.

It was a narrow staircase of dark wood with an old-fashioned feel. Swirling, intricate patterns climbed up the wooden banister, and the ends of the balustrades were carved with claw feet. The wood gleamed richly in the soft light from my bedroom, inviting me to climb it.

I stepped inside, slammed the door shut the door behind me, and started up the stairs. My entire body was vibrating with electric energy, nervous and terrified. *How can this be real?* Maybe I'd fallen asleep waiting. Maybe this was all a dream. That seemed much more likely.

The stairs creaked under my feet. I looked around at the walls—but they were completely nondescript, white walls. I looked down—I couldn't see my closet anymore. I looked up—and saw the glimpse of a door.

I hurried my pace. My hand fell on the doorknob.

I took a deep breath and pushed.

It was my room. My childhood room. The unicorn poster on the wall. The dollhouse in the corner. The bin of dinosaur toys by the bed. And the bed... it was empty.

I looked down at myself—

And realized I was a child.

I ran out of the closet and into the hallway, my little feet pattering on the wooden floor, and peered into my parents room. I saw them sleeping—*both of them.* My mom, turned away from the door, her curly hair in a tangled mess behind her.

My heart swelled.

I didn't sleep a wink. I waited until I heard their footsteps in the hallway—then I bounded out of the room. "Mom!" I screamed.

"Gina," Mom said with a smile. And then both of them sang *happy birthday* to me, grinning from ear to ear.

I couldn't believe it. My mom was here, right in front of me.

And I had the entire day to spend with her.

It was the perfect day. We played board games, saw Eragon, then went out for ice cream. That night they tucked me in, and my mom read me my favorite dinosaur book. I was in heaven.

I almost drifted off in my bed—but then I remembered. The message board had made it clear that each visit was only supposed to be 24 hours. It didn't specify what happened if you stayed longer than that, but I didn't want to find out. So at midnight, I opened the door to my closet—and among the stuffed animals and princess costumes, there was a staircase leading down into the darkness.

The next day sucked. It was like all the color had been sucked out of my world. The only thing that kept me slogging through the day was counting down the minutes to midnight. I'd originally planned to space my tickets out—but as the hours crawled by, I realized I couldn't wait.

So at midnight, I was there again, ready to open the door.

The three days I spent with my parents were the best days of my life. And it wasn't just seeing my mom—to experience life as a kid again, to be ignorant of all the evil in the world and only feel love—it was the most amazing thing I've ever felt. For those three days, my life was sandcastles and Sunday pancakes, morning cartoons and movie nights, unconditional love that didn't waver for a second.

It was the closest thing to true happiness I'd ever felt.

But I knew it had to come to an end. When my mom tucked me in, I fought back tears. I didn't want to upset her. So I told her I loved her, and watched her go. Then, at midnight, I took the ticket off my bookshelf and headed for the closet door. I forced myself to go down the stairs, even though my legs felt like lead.

As soon as I hit the bed, I began to sob.

The following days were difficult. All I could think about was my mother. Spending time with her. And the gnawing sensation at the back of my brain, like a hunger: *I need to go back.*

I still wasn't convinced the whole thing wasn't a dream. The more days that went by between me and the visits, the foggier my memory of them got. It *felt* like I was remembering a dream. Little holes here and there that I couldn't exactly recall. Little details that felt jarringly weird, like dream logic. And the memories always felt just slightly out of my grasp, like they took extra effort to recall.

That didn't change my mind, though. The tickets could be covered in a hallucinogenic powder for all I cared. I needed to go back. *Needed* to.

But when I drove to the corner of Maple and Willow at midnight, the ticket stand wasn't there.

I drove by the next night. And the next. And the next.

It was gone.

My coworkers and friends noticed my change in attitude. I was often late to work, because I'd been up so late the night before driving out to the ticket dispenser. I seemed depressed, I seemed down, and I rarely smiled anymore.

Weeks went by, and I grew more and more resentful. *I made a huge mistake.*

Why didn't I just stay there? I could've stayed there

forever. Screw what the message board said about 24 hours or whatever.

Why didn't I try to bring my mom through the door? Would that even save her, though? Would she still get cancer at the same age? If she followed me, would I be depriving child-me of a mother? Or would she exist in both timelines?

Why did I listen to those stupid rules?

I was just so happy to get anything. A moment. A crumb. Three days felt like a fortune. Now, it felt like nothing.

And then I did something stupid.

I still had the tickets. After each trip, the gold emblem had turned black... but what if I painted it gold again?

I called in sick to work. Then I went to the craft store, picked up some gold paint, and carefully painted over the symbol. Then I waited. My stomach twisted in knots as the clock ticked towards midnight.

I glanced at my phone. 11:55. I got up, legs shaking, and placed the ticket in my back pocket. Then I wrapped my fingers around the closet handle. *11:58... 11:59...*

Go!

I yanked the door open—

And I couldn't believe it. My heart leapt. The staircase was there!

I raced up the steps. I felt like I was flying. *I'm not going to leave this time. I'm going to stay there forever.* My bedroom door came into view above me. I raced faster, desperately reaching out, and pushed it open—

I froze.

The bed wasn't empty. There was me... me, as a child... sleeping in it.

The blood drained from my face. So that was it, then. I couldn't go back. I mean, I could stay here as an adult... but I couldn't go back to being *me*. I stared at myself sleeping, a pang of sorrow hitting me.

That's it.

It's over. I can't go back.

But there was that other option. The totally insane one.

I could bring my mom back with me.

What would happen here, though? Would my mom go missing? Would I not have a mother for the rest of my childhood?

I don't care.

I need to save her. I need to bring her back with me.

I started across the carpeted floor, trying to stay as quiet as possible. I had no idea how I'd get my mom through the door, but I'd do it, somehow. And then we'd be together. She died when I was 14—which meant she had 6 more years to live. *Six years.* Maybe she'd come to my wedding. Maybe she'd meet her first grandchild.

Not just that. Maybe I could get her more advanced medical care. Cancer treatment is always changing, all the time. Maybe she'd live ten years or more in my timeline.

I need to bring her back.

But then I caught my reflection in the window.

And my body went numb.

My face. Everything was in the wrong place. My eyes were skewed away from each other. My jaw was spit down the middle and half of it was tilted, hanging off my neck. Thick, jagged lines sliced across my body, the pieces all shifted and slid away from each other. But there wasn't blood. It wasn't gruesome. I looked... corrupted. Glitched.

I couldn't help it. I screamed.

And me, child-me, shot up in bed. Her eyes flew open. And when she saw me—*she* screamed. Within seconds I heard the footsteps, pounding down the hall.

No no no...

I ran into the closet and slammed the door shut. I leaned against it, holding my breath, my heart pounding in my ears. I looked down—but my arms and legs looked normal, now.

"Mommy," I heard my child-voice cry on the other end. The fear in her voice cut me to the core. "There's a monster in my closet!"

"It's okay, ssshhh." My mom's muffled voice.

"*No!* There's a monster!"

"There's nothing in your closet, sweetie," my mom replied.

"There is! I saw it!"

The footsteps got louder as Mom approached the door. I winced, shutting my eyes tight—I heard the doorknob turn—

"There's nothing in here, sweetie."

I opened my eyes. I could see my mom, clear as day, standing there. But she couldn't see me.

And in that instant, I realized. This was my only chance. If I wanted to bring her back with me... this was it. Before I could even think through my actions—that I was leaving myself motherless, a scared little child—I grabbed her by the arms and pulled her in.

No. No no no.

As soon as she crossed the threshold, it happened.

Her skin was sunken and rotted. Her cheeks were hollow, exposing yellowed bone. Her eyes were pure white, staring blankly into mine. And her arms—they were just bones, barely covered by shriveled bits of skin and tattered clothing.

She was a corpse.

I let go of her. She reeled back—and as soon as she did, her features snapped back to normal. Her shiny, curly hair. Her warm brown eyes. Confusion flashed across her features for a moment. "Huh, I thought…" She trailed off. "Guess I lost my balance there, for a second. But there's nothing in here, sweetie."

I turned around and ran down the stairs. Tears ran down my cheeks. Sobbing, I burst into the room and collapsed on the bed.

I must've fallen asleep, somehow. Because the next thing I knew, bright sunlight was streaming in through the windows.

I forced myself up. Slowly. And looked around.

Where… am I?

The room. It wasn't *my* room. My heart pounded in my ears as I glanced around—there were pictures on the wall I didn't recognize, furniture I'd never seen before—and I was in a king size bed, which meant—

"Oh, you're finally up!"

I looked up to see a man standing in the doorway. A

man I'd never seen before in my life. *Holding the hand of a little girl.*

"Your mommy's up!" he said gleefully. The little girl jumped onto the bed, a big grin on her face. "Mama!" she said proudly. Excitedly.

The stairs brought me back to the wrong time.

No, no, no...

But as I looked at the little girl's face, beaming down at me, I felt something besides shock and fear. That gnawing, horrible feeling that had lived in the back of my brain—that *need* to see my mother, to return to the past—it shifted, slightly. Its claws were not so deeply sunk into my brain anymore. I could see something else, see something past it. Something bright.

I felt myself smile. Just slightly.

"Do you want pancakes?" I asked.

SOS

*Last night, I found an abandoned yacht.
The food was still warm.*

—

We got the distress signal at 8:32 PM.

The signal came via an emergency position-indicating radio beacon (EPIRB), registered a large yacht owned by a man named Daniel Owens. EPIRBs don't send any other information, though, so we had no way of knowing what exactly happened.

"At least the weather's good," I said as we cut across the waves.

"Yeah, but kinda makes you wonder what happened, don't it?" Bobby replied, hands gripping the wheel. "I don't remember the last time we had an SOS without a storm."

"Eh, who knows with these rich fucks," Kim replied, spitting over the side. "They do all kind of weird shit."

The ocean loomed ahead of us, pure darkness pierced only by our headlight. No one ever talks about how *dark* the ocean is—not a single streetlamp, or window, or car to break up the dark. Just pitch black. In every direction.

Well. I could still see the lights from the dock behind us. But it wouldn't be long before they were swallowed up.

I'd been on several search and rescue missions before. Thankfully, they'd all ended well. But Bobby was right—they were all storm-related. Laypeople not knowing the wrath of the ocean. Thinking they can make a little trip into the water for someone's birthday or whatnot when the sky is raging above them and the waves are swelling into mountains.

Respect the ocean, and maybe she won't kill you, my mentor had told me. Those words stuck with me, even a decade later.

And then, before I knew it, we were approaching the yacht. The lights were on, reflecting in the inky black water. Bobby shifted gears and we pulled up to it, slowly, quietly. And that's when I realized how truly massive it was. I'd guess it was a fifty or sixty-footer— easily dwarfing our boat.

Bobby grabbed the megaphone. "US Coast Guard," he said. "Can you hear us?"

Nothing.

Kim and I started with the rope. As we worked, preparing to board, I kept looking up at the yacht; but from the outside, nothing appeared amiss. Golden light bled out of the tinted windows, reflecting placidly on the water. I heard low, instrumental music playing somewhere. I didn't see any damage to the boat, or people in the water.

Kim boarded first. I went next. Bobby stayed in the boat, preparing to search the surrounding water.

Kim slid open the glass door. "After you."

I swallowed and stepped inside.

The doors opened up into a small, but lavishly decorated, room. A kitchenette/bar area stood to the right, and a dining area with tables and booths sat on the left. That's when I noticed the food.

Even though the room was empty, the tables were set with food, as if people had just been there moments before. Glasses of champagne, still bubbling. A filet of salmon, a few bites missing. Lipstick smeared on a napkin.

I pressed my hand to the salmon—and my stomach sank. It was still warm.

They were just *here.*

I glanced at my watch. 8:51 PM. They'd sent the SOS not even twenty minutes ago. How did they go from eating and drinking to just—nothing?

Kim made her way over to me. "I checked below deck. No one's there," she said.

"The food's still warm."

Her eyes widened. "What the hell? Where did they *go?*"

"No idea."

We made our way towards the stairs. Towards the top deck. I doubted we would find them there, but we had to be thorough.

The top deck was open to the air. I glanced at the captain's chair, the steering wheel, the little U-shaped sofa behind them. It was empty. Nothing out of place. "They've got to be in the water," I said grimly. "They're not here, that's for sure."

I looked out below us. At the inky black water, the ripples glinting in the light. I turned, looking around the boat, into the water—

My heart stopped.

"Where's Bobby?"

Our boat was still linked with the yacht. But it was empty.

"Dammit, he must've boarded," Kim snapped, charging for the stairs. "He *never* follows fucking protocol. I always tell him, it's going to get someone killed, but no, he just *has* to do things his way..." Her rant grew muffled as she descended towards the deck.

I followed her.

But Bobby wasn't downstairs. He wasn't in the dining area, or in either of the bedrooms below deck. My heart pounded in my ears as I grew more and more frantic, checking tiny closets that couldn't possibly fit a person, opening the storage cabbies that held the life jackets. "Bobby! Bobby, where are you?!"

A hand clapped over my mouth.

And then something shoved me to the floor. I tried to wrestle away but then I saw a flash of red curls above me—Kim—she was dragging me under the table, whispering, begging me to keep quiet—

Squelch.

Both of us froze. My eyes locked on the source of the

noise—and I saw two rubber boots on the carpet, rivulets of seawater dripping off them.

I glanced up.

Bobby was standing there, in the center of the room.

But something was horribly *wrong* with him.

He was soaking wet, from head to toe. Seawater sloshed in his boots; streams of water ran off his sleeves. His skin was pale and bluish, and there was a patch of white, crusty salt along his jawline, almost reaching his eyes.

And his eyes...

They were pure white. Pupilless. Blank.

Squelch. Bobby took another step. *Squelch.* And another. Kim's nails dug into my arm. We watched as Bobby—no, not Bobby, not anymore—continued walking towards us. I held my breath, shutting my eyes. *Please don't let him see us. Please.*

Squelch.

Two rubber boots. Right in front of our table.

Squelch.

He continued deeper into the cabin.

I let out the breath I was holding. Kim's grip on my arm loosened. As soon as Bobby's steps sounded on the stairs, Kim whispered to me: *"Run."*

I didn't want to. But then she shoved me, *hard,* and I was rolling out from under the table. I scrambled up—just in time to see Bobby freeze on the stairs.

He slowly turned around, his white eyes locking on mine.

I ran. Faster than I'd run in my life. We scrambled out onto the deck, then made our way into the boat, as fast as we could. Kim made it first—then she grabbed my hand, pulling me towards safety—

Squelch.

Bobby's hand locked onto my ankle.

Except they weren't *just* hands. His fingers were jointless, like tentacles, wrapping perfectly around my ankle. Covered in fleshy suction-cups.

And his face—it was rapidly changing. Before my eyes, his salt-encrusted features were morphing, until I saw a woman, then an older man. His flesh squeezing and bloating into its other forms effortlessly, like an octopus squeezing through a tiny hole. But his eyes always stayed the same. White. Blank. Empty.

This is how I die.

But then, with a loud *pop,* I went flying. I crashed into the floor of the boat, pain shooting up my side. By the time I scrambled up, we were several feet away from the yacht, plowing into the ocean.

Back home.

I was so relieved. So thankful. Whatever that thing was, I'd escaped it. I felt better than I had in years. Like all my problems were tiny grains of sand.

But now, I'm not so sure.

Because, this morning—when I looked in the mirror—I noticed my face was encrusted with white flakes of salt.

I BABYSAT A PARROT. IT SAID DISTURBING THINGS

My neighbor, Henry Johnson, would be out of town for two weeks. His wife had just left him, and he needed to clear his head. So he asked me to house sit. As a broke college student, I said yes.

The housesitting duties included taking care of the Johnsons' parrot—a 17-year-old African Grey named Snickers. I didn't know much about birds, but he'd left me detailed instructions on how to take care of her.

The first night of my job, I decided to stay for a few hours. I needed to get a problem set done, and the Johnsons' large, empty house was the perfect study place. After feeding Snickers and giving her water, I got set up on the couch.

But it wasn't long before she interrupted me.

"STOP!"

I whipped around. Snickers was standing on her perch, staring at me with one gray eye. **"STOP! STOP!"** she repeated.

Rolling my eyes, I went back to the problem set. Differential equations. Why did I decide to major in engineering, again? ! tapped my pencil against the page. *Maybe it's time for another snack break.*

"STOP, OH GOD, STOP."

Snickers was bouncing from one perch to the other, bobbing her head, as carefree as could be. But the way she said that sent shivers down my spine. She was clearly imitating someone in distress. *Probably just repeating from a movie,* I told myself.

But I was so, so wrong.

"STOP, OH GOD, STOP. HENRY, STOP."

Henry.

That was his name. Henry Johnson.

I turned and stared at the parrot. She stared back at me and whistled a few times. And them she continued.

"STOP OH GOD STOP HENRY STOP OH GOD"

My blood turned to ice. I stared at the parrot, my heart hammering in my chest. *What, exactly, happened here? What is she repeating?*

I decided to call my parents. But they didn't seem to share my level of concern. "Your Aunt Sheila had a parrot," my dad said. "That thing would pick up all kinds of crazy words. Movies, phone conversations... it'd scream, say the f-word, everything. I wouldn't worry, Abbi. Especially with Raquel leaving him and all... they probably had some huge fights the parrot picked up on. I wouldn't be surprised if it got worse."

And he was right. Over the course of the next hour, Snickers continued to repeat "stop" and "Henry," but also said a variety of other things, from curses to pleasantries to movie quotes. **"FUCK YOU." "I'LL BE BACK." "HOW ARE YOU TODAY?" "COMMENT ALLEZ-VOUS?"**

Finally, around ten o'clock, I started getting ready to leave. Threw my notebook in my backpack, switched off the lights, and headed for the door. "Goodbye Snickers," I called out into the darkness. Then I reached for the doorknob—

"PUT THE KNIFE DOWN."

I froze in my tracks.

I couldn't see Snickers anymore. But I could hear her, rustling about in her cage. Talons clacking against the metal rails, feathers flapping in the silence. *Maybe she's just quoting another movie. Maybe she's—*

"PUT THE KNIFE DOWN HENRY," the bird repeated.

My heart dropped.

"STOP OH GOD STOP OH GOD."

Snickers was agitated. I could hear her feathers hitting the metal rails of her cage as she flapped her wings. *Thunk*—she hopped back and forth, perch to perch, as she clicked her beak erratically.

"STOP OH GOD STOP."

I stood there for a long time. Seconds stretched into minutes. But she didn't say anything more. Just clicked and whistled and flapped around in her cage.

I flicked the lights back on, dropped my backpack on the floor, and made a beeline for the Johnsons' bedroom.

Henry was very clear with his instructions. I wasn't supposed to enter any of the bedrooms or the basement. I was supposed to stay on the main level, no matter what.

But I climbed the stairs anyway. After looking around, I found their bedroom. It was neat and tidy, the burgundy bedspread laying smoothly over the mattress. I walked around, my heart hammering, hoping what I was imagining wasn't true.

But it was.

Because in their closet, I found a small box. A small box containing Raquel Johnson's wallet... and drivers license.

I made my way back down the stairs, my legs shaking. Snickers looked at me curiously from her cage. I turned out the lights, locked the door, and hurried down the sidewalk. *As soon as I get home, I'm calling the cops. As soon as I—*

Ping.

I pulled out my phone to see a text.

From Henry Johnson.

I asked you not to enter the bedroom.

I whipped around. But the dark sidewalk extended behind me, totally empty. *How did he... Oh. A camera. Of course.* I broke into a run towards my parents' house, at the corner. *Almost there—*

Ping.

I know what you saw.

I sprinted harder, faster. My feet slapped against the pavement. *Almost there—*

Ping.

I didn't pull out my phone. Didn't stop until I was locked safely in my parents' house. Then, finally, I read the text that he sent.

If you tell anyone else, you will pay.

I didn't listen. I called the police. And after a thorough search of his house, they found something horrible.

Raquel's body, in the freezer in the basement.

Henry was trying to flee town, but get a head start by making it look like he was just going on vacation. So he hired me to housesit. I don't think he realized Snickers might repeat what she heard that night.

And sometimes, I wonder, if Snickers knew more than she let on. Because, apparently, she was Raquel's pet. From before they were even married.

Maybe she wasn't mindlessly repeating.

Maybe she was trying to get justice for Raquel.

The nightmares continue in...

PRE-ORDER NOW
Available April 15, 2024

I hacked someone's Ring camera. I saw something horrifying.

There's something wrong with the moon.

I deliver letters to dead people.

Has anyone heard of the "Bloodworth Incident?" Everyone in my town is talking about it, but they won't tell me what actually happened...

LET ME IN brings you 30 terrifying tales for your darkest nights. This collection has every flavor of horror, from terrifying nightshift jobs to strange dogs, from disturbing videos online to foreboding letters. Read... if you dare.

Hungry for more horror? Visit www.blairdaniels.com or sign up for my newsletter.

Thanks for reading!

Printed in Great Britain
by Amazon